Where is my place in this world?

From egotistical to altruistic way of existence.

This book explains how to move above and beyond one's conditioning to get access to an unrepressed and infinite state of being where one can see that everything is inner connected and there is no separation. To get there one must increase her level of understanding and put her life to practice. The more one experiences life with awareness and knowledge, the closer she gets to her wholeness and that unlimited potential she beholds.

Roya R. Rad

Order this book online at www.trafford.com
or email orders@trafford.com

Most Trafford titles are also available at major online book retailers.

Disclaimer

The publisher and the author make an effort to give valid information to the public, however, they make no guarantee with respect to the accuracy or completeness of the contents of the books published. Science is unlimited and there are many facts yet to be discovered and improved upon, as the world expands. The information that SKBF Publishing presents to the public can only be used as a personal enhancing device for building a healthy life style. The reader is always responsible for using the information the best possible way according to his or her unique needs, environment and personality. Books, lectures, websites and other forms of self help tools are general and valuable tools for a person looking for self education but, sometimes, they are more like statistical information. They will give us a general idea about most people but we have to remember that each of us is a unique individual and treatment for our healing process would have to be administered accordingly.

Printed in Victoria, BC, Canada.

ISBN: 978-1-4269-2519-1 (sc)

ISBN: 978-1-4269-2830-7 (hc)

Our mission is to efficiently provide the world's finest, most comprehensive book publishing service, enabling every author to experience success. To find out how to publish your book, your way, and have it available worldwide, visit us online at www.trafford.com

Trafford rev. 1/13/2010

Edited by: Walter L. Kleine, Kleine Editorial Services
All poems by Roya R. Rad

Published in USA by SKBF Publishing www.SKBFPublishing.com

Trafford PUBLISHING® *www.trafford.com*

North America & international
toll-free: 1 888 232 4444 (USA & Canada)
phone: 250 383 6864 • fax: 812 355 4082

Contents

Dedication

For Dave, who opened up a door of pure bond.

For my sons, Peter (Pedram) and Paul (Parham) who add a glow to my life.

For my parents who carried me when they could, and when they didn't, it was simply because they didn't know how.

For all the people whose genuine acts have moved and touched me one way or the other, big or small, from a sincere smile to a life-enhancing advice or act. For their true encouraging words and caring actions, for making it easier for me to feel onestep closer to my essence, since they revealed theirs to me.

To the people who crossed my path who would never know how much I admired them because I concealed it. To the ones whom I craved an exchange of a hug just meeting them, but had to hold back because I didn't want to make them feel uncomfortable.

To the ones I see for the first time, but sense that inner connection as if we knew each other before. I wish I could say it to all of those as it was, but the world is not there yet. We are not ready to hear it as it is, we may take it the wrong way, we may get scared, we may feel overwhelmed, or threatened. If someone just showed too much affection too quickly, we may feel confused, since we may not be used to it. We may have seen others do it to us, usually out of impulsivity or some form of manipulation. So, our mind has to be trained to see it as is. I celebrate that day when it comes, and will walk out giving whoever inspires me a hug, I will let them know they did, but until then, I will just keep it within and use my writing to unleash my inner feelings.

Mind Stimulation

It's time to stop separating things, and start thinking about how they can go together.

We have to experience having a complete sense of self to learn how to become selfless. That comes with learning and experiencing. The more complete the sense of self, the more transparent the state of selflessness.

Evolution was created, and creation is evolving.

Dark and light are the continuation of the same spectrum. We tend to separate them due to our conditioning. Dark is a separation from light, and light is a connection to the source.

All concepts, including those of science and religion, should evolve as we are moving forward, or they may turn into confusing obstacles instead of helpful means.

Everything we do up to the point of self-authentication and self actualization is for self-interested reasons. Whether we are aware of it or not does not change the truth of it, denying it will only make the process more unclear.

The only thing that makes a human being more advanced is how close she is getting to her source of higher self and how closely she is moving toward her full potential. The rest are nothing more than subjective conditioning and personal preferences.

If we are giving our self credit for doing a good deed, we may need to think and evaluate it again. When our higher self is doing something, there is no credit to be taken; it is a natural process. An authenticated self has an innate structure of giving; one just has to get there. Giving comes in many different sizes, shapes, and forms, and cannot be measured by outside factors and in terms of quantity.

Sometimes, the best way to give to the world is not to take more than needed, and not to leave a negative impact.

As we evolve, we can see how everything is inner-related. It starts from the inner and goes all the way to the outer layer, but they all end at the same place. Repressing or suppressing one element of our self and that of others will create nothing more than resentment and negativity that will shape the whole picture. We are only beginning to see the long-term consequences of our actions and not just the short term gratifications of the lower self, or the ego. We are finally starting to see beyond the tip of the iceberg, we are asking why, we are looking for the truth behind what we are being told, we are starting to show the ability to comprehend and understand without being manipulated by external factors, and that is why an era of global awareness may be closer than we think.

It is not what we see, but where it is rooted. Courage, pride, loyalty, assertion, connection, self-value, etc., if coming from the lower self, may not be what they present themselves to be, since the lower self can become the master of manipulation. We get the truth of what is only if it comes from the higher self. Self-evaluation is the key.

We need to learn that it is not the behavior, but the intent behind the behavior, that matters.

We start from a point, we understand and experience to the fullest, we go back to the same point.

We need to learn about what we hold, understand, and accept, and move beyond it. We need to understand that what we hold is not who we are. It is only an object, like many others, for us to learn who we are. We cannot turn an object into a goal; that would be limiting. Only after understanding comes liberation to move above and beyond. Anything before that is nothing more than avoidance, repression and denial.

Giving our inner child the parental balance of love and discipline it may lack is a first step to wholeness.

One has to practice ways to become self-disciplined and shape her being before finding the ability to become self-liberated. Liberation is not an external sense, but an inner freedom. It is a stage in which one is not a slave of any external circumstances and is given the privilege of being the master of her own existence. It is the freedom to be in charge of one's destiny by having full access to our free will.

Anytime you judge something too harshly, try to learn about it. You may just be surprised.

Being run by emotions creates impulsivity. Impulsive reactions are usually unproductive. Emotions and feelings are signals, nothing more; they are not to be given too much power. They have to be attended to, experienced, and listened to, but after that we are the ones who should be in charge.

Irrational thinking and ignorance can spread like a disease from individuals to nations, and vice versa. They are rooted in wickedness, and create a self-feeding cycle. We may get to a point where we create illusive facts to support our irrational thinking. The less civilized a society, the more ignorance it experiences; it is a limiting element. The ones suffering from this disease get defensive if truth comes along threatening their comfort zone, and will do anything possible to protect the garbage they hold on to. For too long, we have been trying to use the right words to explain the situation. The right word is nothing more than the truthful word.

The more closed the mind, the more rigid the self, and the more defensive and opinionated the person holding that self. Such a person creates a small world with all elements needed to nourish this limited way of being. She makes it impossible for the truth to enter the door; the door is almost made of iron. The truth waits patiently behind the door until she is ready to open it.

Until we get to a point where we learn that what we see may not be what we get, we keep on chasing our own tail.

There has to be a balance between the material world and that of the unseen. If we focus too much on one and not the other, we cannot have the whole experience. We cannot deny or avoid something that exists, and need to understand that there is a reason for its existence. Until we experience it, we will not be able to find out that the reason may be.

Our creator has given us the power to create, all the way to infinity. We can even re-create our own self.

If you release something without understanding and experiencing it, you are avoiding or denying its existence, and that can lead to repression and drawback. However, if you release something after you understand and experience it, and move above and beyond it, you have outgrown it.

What is this book all about?

To tell you what this book is about, I will start with what this book is *not* about. This book is not about either of the extreme sides of the spectrum. It is not for those who are looking for how to "feel" good all the time, but for those who want to discover how to "be" full and find contentment, which by itself creates a balanced state of feeling. It is also for those self-seekers who are not interested in the surface and want to know the root of their feelings, emotions, and thoughts, and use that knowledge to grow.

In addition, it offers ways to understand being content, not continuously spending time and effort in finding instant gratifications. Too many times, too many of us spend a large portion of our valuable time looking for a sense of quick pleasure, or impulsive and short term relief, that has no real effect on the quality of our lives and making progress. Even though pleasure is an important part of life, it shouldn't be leading our way. We should be in charge, not the other way around. If we let impulses control us, we may feel like we are working around a circle, from one point to the same point, without accomplishing or building as much as we could. Impulses don't have the ability to take into account the short- and long-term consequences, and only look for a quick sense of gratification, not considering that for every benefit there is a price to be paid. They come from our more primitive nature. It is time to really think. Is the price we are paying worth the benefit we are receiving, and, even further, are we even receiving any benefits? And then ask why, or why not? A simple question that opens the door to awareness.

The book will not discuss how to be in a state of all happiness, since this could encourage a sense of escape from reality. Life is a combination of everything; sometimes painful events and sometimes joyful ones. It is not the event or the feeling associated with it that matters, it is what we get out of it and what we take from it. We cannot walk a healthy life by escaping from the reality that we may have to experience some pain if we have a life worth living. Having an irrational fear of experiencing pain will create a person who would do anything to avoid that experience. If we overlook that simple rule, we will spend a lifetime feeling like we are chasing our own tail rather than moving upward.

For all of us, there is work to be done. There are no quick fixes. Anything worth having needs a lot of work. What is more precious than having a fulfilled life and connecting with our source? The more valuable something is, the more focus and effort it takes to gain it.

When we deny reality, deny facts, escape or avoid feeling any kind of pain at all costs; we shape ourselves for living a life that is getting farther from the truth. We don't want to hear the reality. We become defensive if anyone challenges our fantasy land. Meantime, we want to do anything to get a sense of happiness, not even knowing what it means for us. If we don't know who we are, we don't know what happiness means to us, since happiness has many meanings, depending on the stage we're at. Our definition of happiness becomes what others tell us happiness should be, we go back to our primate form, and we imitate others rather than following our build-in guidance.

We will need to understand our feelings and emotions as being as much a part of us as our hands and legs. Just because we cannot see something does not mean it does not exist. If we start paying attention, we will notice what a big part these two elements play in our daily life and how we react to situations. We can learn to recognize what they are trying to communicate with us, where they are coming from, respond to them, process them and act to balance them. Again, if we ignore or avoid them, we are giving them control. But, if we pay attention to the signals they are giving us, we can find a way to deal with them rather than being engulfed by them. So, they are, in a way, tools as a package given to us for this process we call life.

Our goal in life may be to learn about ourselves and our surroundings and walk toward a state of full potential, being as productive as we can be, having the least negative impact, and having the most positive one before our departure. Remember, with every breath we take, we are one breath closer to death, so how are we managing our life, and what is our intention of living it? The more we get obsessed over feeling good at all times and stay away from learning about the process, the more we will find ourselves looking for external sources of happiness. The more we do that, the harder it gets to feel happy, since the source of happiness comes from a place right within us, once we start paying attention. It is from in to out rather than out to in. If we find a way of reversing this process, we may very well find the happiness we are looking for. But we have to follow the rules first.

Throughout this book, we discuss learning as an important means by which one can expand and find a sense of inner balance. It is important to note that learning and happiness go hand in hand, like the chicken-egg example. The more we learn about ourselves and our surroundings, the more we may be able to find our true sources of happiness, based on who we are and what we want. The more we feel happy, the more we are able to learn. There is no separation; they complete each other.

It is time for us to look at the glass of half-filled water as it is; neither all full nor all empty, but half and half. Irrational optimism could be as off-putting as too much pessimism. Seeing things as close to their truth as possible is the most productive way to go, seeing the reality as it is with all that it offers. Escaping from what brings pain will not be the road to finding joy. As advancing and evolving minds, we are learning that we have spent too much time separating things that are really complementary to each other. We like to get into these games of making things go into a resistance mode rather than working as allies. We want to make up a delusional reality, and then fight hard to prove that it is the right and only one. We work from a selfish state of mind, "If it belongs to me, it has to win or be better." Now, let's think about it, night and day complete each other, they don't really go against each other, right? We can't say night is bad or day is good. We may have preferences due to personal habits and conditioning but if we look at it logically, we can't say because we prefer day that it is better. We know one cannot be without the other. These two are working hand in hand to give us a sense of timing. The same applies to many other things we try so hard to separate. It is us humans who continuously want to put things that belong together in opposition, creating negativity. We act selfishly, and blind ourselves to the truth.

It's time for us to stop numbing ourselves from the pain and investing time in pain relievers. Let's find the source of pain and start the healing process. To do that, we have to grow a love of learning, start to self-reflect, and look for the deeper truth behind what is seen. This is an everlasting process. We have to open our minds to receive new information, including new factual information about different subjects, cultures, new ideas, new beginnings, and different perspectives. The more we learn and apply the learning, the more we feel a sense of inner expansion. Black-and-white thinking is a thing of close mindedness; an open mind can see that things work on a continuum and affect each other constantly.

This information may already be within you; you just need to learn to connect. Last, there is a great deal to be learned from failure. If we only focus on achievement, we may fail to benefit from a good opportunity.

Is Psychology The New Spirituality?

I have heard it many times from many people that they are looking into modern science, including multimodal psychology and quantum physics, searching for answers to spirituality. It is as if our mind's evolution is not satisfied with what we don't understand. We have moved above the imitation and ritualistic stage into an era of thirst for understanding. A more mature mind looks for answers to "why," and "how," rather than emulating rituals and following others. Development does not fit into being a sheep.

There is, however, this red flag. While people seem to have more and more of a thirst for psychology, at the same time some tend to run from it because they may think it is too knotty or analytical. For that reason, I have made it my goal to combine stories with simple and lucid language to make psychology as unfussy as possible. I will try to introduce psychology as a people's science and a new way of spirituality, finding a bridge between the two that can be crossed without too much fear. The more bridges we can build between things we separate, the shorter and easier our way will become. Our free will has an integrated choice of doing what we want and putting together what works. How do we want to use it?

While we are trying to use our free will to choose the path of life that will be most productive for our unique process of growth, we cannot help noticing that there are many distractions. It takes a well-informed, skillful, experienced, well-built, strong and evolved mind to be able to resist superfluous temptations and keep focusing and moving forward. It would be less painful and demanding for us to walk the path if we walk with a light baggage, carrying only what we need and letting go of what we don't. Hauling burdensome and heavy baggage, full of irrational, out of balance, and unproductive thoughts, feelings, and behaviors, in addition to too many grudges of the past and worries of the future, will do nothing but to slow us down and hurt us.

We may be doing ourselves a service if we become more awake and conscious of the fact that our religion, culture, ethnicity, education, family background, country, etc., are not really making us better or worse than others. They are just elements of our existence and means by which we can achieve our goal of self-growth. Sure, there are some countries that have more civilized environments than others, but what we, as an individual, make of our self using the means that we have is what values us as a human being, not the means itself. Valuing the means alone as a way of thinking is no different than thinking we are prettier than others because our shoes are more expensive. Now, how silly does that sound? So, as I said, all of these are means by which we can get the resources we need to make the travel through this path of life more fruitfully. If we start the distracting process of categorizing humans as superior or inferior based on external factors, just to feel better about ourselves without deserving it, and to fill our own inner voids, we may be wasting a lot of valuable time and energy on negative forces rather than positive ones. It is not about what means and surroundings we have, but what we do with what we have that makes us who we are. If we are not working hard to make the best of what we have, we cannot take much credit for possessing it. On the other hand, we are even more to blame if we have a good means and do not have the ability to make good use of it.

Means and tools are not for unhealthy competitions but are to be used for growth. We cannot just give ourselves a status based on a tool we have without working hard toward gaining that status with integrity and honesty. For example, if one's tool is that she is intelligent, that, by itself, does not make that person any more advanced than others if she doesn't use that intelligence to create something positive and to help herself grow. Or, even worse, if such a person uses that intelligence to feed the ego (tip of the iceberg), or to make something harmful, she has wasted or misused her power and has walked away from her full integrity and potential. Integrity and potential are built-in traits that need to be acknowledged. If one walks away from them, she is walking away from her truth. The further we get from our truth, the less value we posses.

We humans spend so much power trying to demonstrate to each other that we are better or superior in some external way that we really don't even know why we are doing it. It has become a habit that does not serve us. We can't help but think that if that energy was focused more on real self-growth, we would all be better off. Even animals and plants seem to know their roles. It seems like they just come and go about doing what they are supposed to do. We, on the other hand, focus so much on the image that we may forget the real thing.

Imagine we are climbing a mountain. We put a lot of energy and determination into getting to the top, not with the intention of winning but with the intention of enjoying and having a sense of discovery. Now, as we get to the top, we stand at the summit and look down, Our vision has expanded and we can see more. We cannot help noticing this astonishing beauty and coordination of nature that every single plant contributes to. At the summit, there is no separation; all we see is harmony. The trees look more and more like they are complementing each other, while when you were looking at them from ground level they seemed different from each other. From the ground, one was greener and taller, and they all had different shapes and types. Looking from the top, the plants are not spending time trying to prove to each other that one is better than the other. I know that sounds silly but bear with me and you will get my point. We don't see an aspen birch wanting to be a Douglas fir or vice versa. They seem to innately have their position and role set, and are content with that. And it makes us wonder, are our free will and evolved thought process curses or blessings? The answer lies at the heart of the question: our free will gives us the choice of whatever we want to make of it.

We need to stop comparing ourselves with others and continuously trying to manipulate our mind. There is a lot of work that still needs to be done, and only we can accomplish that. We have all heard that the grass is greener at the neighbors. The reason is that we see it from a distance and don't really see the weeds, while with our grass we see every detail. It won't be a fair comparison, since we don't know the deep truth. If only we could keep our focus away from others, judging them, talking about them, trying to be like them, trying to get what they have, trying to be better than them, interfering with their life, projecting our inner voids on them, finding some flaws in them to make ourselves feel better about our own flaws, or on the other side of the spectrum, idealizing them and having unreasonable expectations from them. Most of us do one or more of these behaviors consciously or unconsciously, leaving some negative impact. If only we could turn the camera on ourselves, acknowledge and accept it, and start the discovery process; a process that goes all the way to infinity. Walking a couple of miles down the road would not cut it. So, which one will we choose, this endless process or that wasteful one?

We should stop for a minute and ask ourselves, why is it that we spend a lifetime running away from ourselves and toward a state of nothingness? Why is it that we have such a deep fear of ourselves? Why is it that we neglect the essence and spend so much time on the worthless? Why is it that we focus on the tip of the iceberg and fail to see the deep? And why is it that we feel like we are chasing our own tail, running in a circle instead of climbing up? And why is it that we keep repeating words as if they don't mean anything?

Then we come to think that maybe we are not here just to finish a degree, be rich, or have a family of our own, though all these are great accomplishments, which can help in building a stronger sense of identity and responsibility while helping us discover the wholeness we behold. But with an inapt use, they will be nothing more than another food for the ego. Then we think, we may be here to mature and develop emotionally, intellectually, mentally, and spiritually, all of which go hand in hand. These are all reflections of each other, and the more transparent we become, the more we can realize that they are parts of the same body, the deeper they go, and the more transparent they become.

In addition, it is important to consider that if we develop in one aspect and not the other, the balance will be jeopardized, and sometimes even disastrous. For example, if we are developed intellectually but immature emotionally, the result of this disparity can be limiting. It is like the intellectual whose ego is so inflated that she does not want to give herself a chance to see that emotionally she is impulsive and childish. Therefore, she closes the door to further growth.

It is also worth questioning ourselves by asking, is what we are chasing not the ultimate objective but the channel by which the objective is to be reached? And if so, why is it that in the process we got confused and forgot about the real objective?

Maybe that is why we see more anxiety, stress, relationship problems, conflicts, manipulation, inner anger, depression, and simple ignorance than we would like to. It's time to be honest about it and stop trying to deny the facts or be unreasonably optimistic. The evolving mind demands honesty, even if it hurts or does not sound comforting. The evolving mind is not looking at hearing what feels good, but what is the truth, because the truth is what feels good. We are, in some ways, tired of those who try to give an image of positivity and optimism without giving us the real deal. We are getting smarter and are learning to see the force behind the persona. It is not about the behavior anymore, but the intention behind it. There is work that must be done, and the first step is for us to admit to the truth.

Some people estimate that we may be at the peak of the above issues, and there comes a time that we will get tired of them and will decide that we want to take a different route. That is why an era of more awareness may be closer. An era of awareness that helps closed minds expand, an era in which true inner compassion, not a phony expression, comes to place. An era where understanding replaces anger. An era in which there is no narrow thinking that one is better or superior because of a certain ethnicity, culture, religion, or other external factors. An era in which how you are valued is who you truly are, not your external features, images, and behaviors. It would be harder and harder to fool a continuously evolved mind. As we become deeper, we see deeper, as we become evolved, we see a more expanded picture. Narrow-mindedness is a disease that brings about destruction. There comes a time when we see the baggage we're carrying and decide, I have been given this one life. I'd better not walk it with so much extra/unneeded/wasteful stuff, since it is slowing down my walk and bending me down to the ground.

But first, we all have to make a collective decision to really try to see if there is something we're missing, some way of thinking, belief, or behavior that is holding us back. When we get used to a comfort zone and feel indolent about moving forward, our mind plays tricks on us. We start a process of self-talk and filtration to support our hypothesis that there is no need for us to step out or go deeper. Many times, we don't walk out of the comfort zone because of the fear of unknown, rejection, uncertainty, etc. Fear, like any other emotion, when reasonable, is needed for survival, but unreasonable fear is nothing more than an obstacle. It is time to see what our reason for stopping is, and start the process.

I will end this chapter with an end note about the state of wholeness, accepting who we are and what we are made of. Wholeness if a combination of opposites, anything and everything. Self-discovery involves acknowledging all there is to us, including strength and weaknesses. Only then we can build on the strength and make the weakness stronger. Only then we will be in charge of our own reality. But we can't manage what we don't acknowledge and accept, and we certainly cannot change what we deny. What we avoid and deny, we repress and make denser, what we repress can control us.

Wholeness

My beauty is that I am all that I am
I avoid the false and the sham

I am both shadow and light
I am both slave and knight

I am both center and edge
I am both water and ledge

When I go to the center, I feel strong
When I go to the edge, I feel wrong

I am what I am, good and bad
I have all the feelings, happy and sad

I go out, I come in
I wonder constantly

It is my destiny to find what is within me
There is no end

It goes all the way to infinity
There is no mystery, the mystery is within me

It is my boundary that keeps me steady
It is my awareness that makes me ready

Poem by Roya R. Rad

A Touch Of Personal Background

In this chapter, I will discuss some of my family background and how my life's pattern escorted me to where I am today. I will combine this experience with my educational background in psychology, as well as my professional life as a researcher, to bring information that may be useful to the reader. Reading this book, you may notice that we humans have many more things in common than we think. Then it almost seems ridiculous that we focus on the tip of the iceberg, and get into selfish conditionings of fighting over who gets more and feeling superior, while we are missing a whole state of existence that is nothing more than magnificent. Now, I am not deserting the fact that even at this tip of the iceberg, there are circumstantial differences that may affect us, but with awareness, we are in the driver's seat, not being driven, but driving.

Moving deeper into the truth, there may come a time when we realize that we need to understand whatever we behold and move beyond it. We may know many who are on either side of the spectrum, either idealizing or amplifying what they have or being ashamed and running away from it. Both are rooted in repressing forces within, which need some digging into, but to get to the point of this chapter, while some people tend to over-identify themselves, based on their race, religion, family background, ethnicity, etc., others may completely deny these factors and hold them back. However, there is a middle point in which we need to understand our elements, accept, pick and choose what works and what needs to outgrow, and move forward. Anything beside this middle point is nothing more than a limiting factor.

Being born in a Muslim family in Iran, and living the majority of my life in US, I have come to realize that I am moving farther and farther away from being an Iranian, an American, a combination, a Muslim, or anything else. I am feeing myself from certain categorizations, and am starting to have a more generalized sense of existence. I have even come to move above being just a mother, a doctor, or all these other labels I used to give myself. The more I am able to do that, the more liberated I feel and the more connected I get to my surroundings. That helps a sense of inner balance that replaces anxious attachments with pure love.

Moving above something does not mean it holds no place in you. On the other hand, the more you learn about something, the more you learn to value it from a rational perspective rather than a black and white way of thinking. You value what is valuable and admit and let go of the flaws. When we are to reach our wholeness, we realize that we are much more than just one or two elements, and that is, in a way, a selfish way of looking at things. This can help prevent us from closing our eyes to the truth and looking deeper. When one can see below the surface, it gets harder to be a black and white thinker. As we become more rationalized and expanded in our perspectives, our level of selfless understanding increases, and we may find ourselves able to experience life more fully, since we are not limiting our selves based on conditioned categorizations. We find ourselves not taking issues on a personal level but from a more truth-oriented level. We find ourselves having a little of everything, and this is an indescribable sense of liberation.

To touch on the personal side a little more, the city in Iran where I was born was one of the smaller cities, we were a well-respected family in the community. My mom was a well-educated woman who was not ordinary in that environment and at the time, so she was unique. This, however, has changed and the number of women who are getting an education is increasing significantly. My father was a successful businessman who had a reputation for being a man of integrity. My paternal grandfather was a lawyer, and then a judge, in the city, and had a street named after him due to the respect and trust he had in society. However, he did have two wives, which was not as out of ordinary as it is today in the more modern Iran. I had a large number of aunts and uncles, and since my dad was the oldest of the brothers, there was a great deal of family attachment as well as pressure, responsibility and expectations. This was a blessing as well as a weight. The blessing was that I experienced a great sense of love during my childhood. Being the only girl in the family for a while, the attention I received fulfilled me in many ways, but the pressure was that individuation was out of question. No one wanted their comfort zone to be threatened, and it would need someone with a lot of courage to step out of what she thought was not functional for her.

During my teenage life, Iran went through a lot of changes, which created unbearable instability. Before it could heal from the damages of revolution, there was a war. The whole country and its residents went through a re-traumatization before they could realize they were traumatized the first time. It was not an easy task to be a teenager during that time. In addition, the fact that I was a young woman, expected to be a picture-perfect image of being classy, having prestige, and behaving well at all times did not help me in my learning process, since I was not allowed to make mistakes and was not encouraged showing my true feelings. I was given the task of being a role model without even knowing why and how. It was not uncommon in families to take it as a sign of disrespect to say something that parents did not approve of, it was not elegant to be assertive, and it was certainly not tasteful to have any sense of unconventionality. The smaller the city, the more these rules applied, and my city was somewhere in the middle. At about 19, I moved to US, marrying someone I did not know that well and did not feel a connection with. After that, I tried to be successful but always felt like something was missing. Little did I know that "something" was my sense of individuality and creativity that I had put to sleep during my teenage life. Avoiding it sure did not help. It wasn't going anywhere just because I was ignoring it. It was only getting bigger, trying really hard to get out. It was giving me signals through anxiety and other inner feelings, but I was not paying attention. Only after full-blown emotional pain did I start to pay attention to the signals.

How I started to pay attention is quite another story. I had to calm my extrovert side a little and pay more consideration to the introvert one. Since I was raised in a crowded family, my extrovert side was quite functional. However, the introvert was neglected. Finding that balance point was a challenge, but quiet worth it. To do this, I went through a phase of seclusion, but not a typical corner of the world or cave in the mountain seclusion. The seclusion I went through was more a matter of cutting back on the unnecessary noise. I was still quite involved with my advocacy and volunteer work, my education, and in my children's activities, but I cut back from my hectic social life and other things that I knew could have a mind effect on me. I wanted to quiet the outside noise and pay attention to the inside.

Once I found that change needed to be made, I was serious about starting the process. The more I learned not to be apprehensive of what I hold, the more I learned to enjoy spending time with myself, a time of self-reflection which brought great rewards. As I learned about myself, a sense of inner liberation started to set in. As if I was more and more walking into an endless experience, I was experiencing my being. I was not just an observer. I was a full participant.

It is astonishing how mind and psych work. It seems like the more we escape from pain, the more we're drowned in it. The more we're fearful of something, the more we face it. This goes on and on. This is obvious in daily life as well. For example, I was listening to a dog trainer talking about how if we are scared of a dog, we would actually increase our chances of attracting the dog because our body gives signals telling the dog that this person is paying attention. Sure, it's negative attention, but it is indeed attention, so the dog is more likely to come toward the one who is experiencing fear.

If we really pay attention and be aware of the present, gain knowledge, apply the knowledge, and if we stop living with the baggage of our past and in worry of the future, then we can see that there is an orderly mechanism to life. A mechanism that is accessible to everyone to learn about. The basis of this mechanism seems to be that any unbalanced and unproductive thought, feeling, emotion, and behavior will bring about an obstacle to growth. The greater this is out of balance, the more elevated the obstacle. If we analyze this, we see an undeniable truth to it. I will discuss this in more detail throughout the book.

While we are growing up, we tend to pick up elements of our environment. Some of these elements are productive while others may not be. A thought, behavior, or habit that may have worked for someone we know may not work for us. So, it is important that we analyze and evaluate our upbringing to see what we are carrying, to keep on carrying what works and to get rid of what does not. This process cannot be over- or under-estimated.

The more we pay attention and experience awareness, the more we live from within, the more we work from within, the more in control we feel. The outside world is unlimited, and can become confusing if we focus on it. The inside world, however, is within reach, and we can learn to manage it. We can get to a point in which we feel in charge of our thoughts, emotions, behaviors, etc. When we sense a feeling of inner control, there is less need for controlling others. Focusing on the inner world's needs means letting go of unneeded distractions, which brings about more focus, which leads to the ability to live a more fulfilled life through accomplishing goals.

When it comes to happiness, we may have seen people who report being happy, but are not doing much to get to their full potential. We may also have noticed that some people report feeling happiness because they are detached from their emotional state and do not know what to make of it. They may confuse having no feelings as being happy. So, we come to the question of what happiness means. We may come to realize that life is more about living fully, and that "fully" does not mean having a continual sense of instant gratification. On the other hand, to be able to truly find the meaning of one's life, one has to learn how to delay gratification and take into consideration the long- and short-term effects of responding to impulses.

If we all get to our full state of functioning, there would be no negative impact on us, people around us, and our surroundings. Most of us have some form of negative impact without realizing it. The luckiest of us are those who are aware of this, and have some form of conscious attention to their actions. The unluckiest ones are those who have a negative impact, but give it a positive image and believe their own lie. This is a form of self-manipulation. Sometimes, people practice it so much that they become masters of it. Manipulation, with the sole intent of self-interest, is the most dangerous form of human interaction, because we may not know what is coming at us.

We have all seen people who are so engulfed by the image that they completely distance themselves from who they really are. Their definition of happiness changes, their definition of joy changes, and their ego becomes their total self. They walk an empty life. Even worse, such individuals may surround themselves with people who feed their ego. When it comes to people, quantity is much easier than quality, so an ego-feeder can easily manage to surround herself with a large number of people who support her views. Such a person wants attention at all costs. Wanting to get attention, the right time, the right way, and the right amount is normal and not a bad thing, but it is the concept of obsession and being out of balance that damages whoever gets into the mess. Feeding one's lower self or the ego can go on forever. The more we feed it, the hungrier and more inflated it becomes. It may take us to a point where we forget that there is something deeper that also needs to be attended to much more than the shallow.

We may wonder why we feel empty, shallow, stressed, despaired, and lonely, even while surrounded by many, and dissatisfied. We do more and more to use some form of external factor to not feel that way, and wonder why it is not working, not knowing that this is a cycle that has no mercy on us once we are in it. After all, why should it, when we don't have mercy on ourselves? If we do not do self-reflection to see that this image is just a persona, a surface, we may be trapped in this vicious cycle of illusion until all the energy we hold is drained out of our existence, all the way to a state of nothingness. What a waste of the precious self!

To end this chapter, as an Iranian-American, Muslim-born woman, at the beginning of my self-growth and awareness process I would ask myself, "Where is my place in this world?" I found myself getting bothered by what I saw as lack of knowledge and mind limitation. In addition, I found myself feeling offended by one group's intolerance or narrow-mindedness toward the other, which seemed to be a widespread problem. I didn't feel like I could feel comfortable with any group. So, I thought, if my views keep on moving forward, would I be getting more and more isolated? Little did I know that as I moved forward with learning and self-practice, and as my awareness expanded, not only did I not become more isolated, but also I became more adjusted to the fact that I actually belong with all the groups. Now, I am learning to be able to see that most people have something good to offer, if we allow them to do so. The ignorance comes from their limited experience, not from their totality. I am learning to enjoy the benefits of interacting with each group, and can filter out what does not work for me and my way of thinking. I look at it with more compassion; a compassion that is more of an inner feeling than an outer doing. I still have my preferences and clear boundaries, especially when it comes to my core values, but I don't internally react to those who are different. My sense of where do I belong has more or less changed than moved to understanding that I am somehow a part of all. That, along with discovering and functioning from a whole self rather than a restricted one, my sense of fear of loneliness has completely vanished. It is literally nonexistent, and a self-energizing experience.

As a result of this growth, I have come to have access to many opportunities that I would have missed otherwise, awakening opportunities. Momentous interaction with different people from all kind of backgrounds, finding deep and meaningful relationships, and finding love are just some of these. I can't see myself building such a sense of fulfillment if my mind was set on conditionally-held irrational beliefs, stereotyping, and categorization. I don't think I would have a fraction of what I have if I had limited myself like that. There is so much out there, but only if we open up. There are hidden diamonds in every culture, race, country, ethnicity and religious background, and if we stick to one little corner, we miss out a whole lot. What a waste would that be!

Tranquility

To feel that inner sense of tranquility
One has to learn a state of inner stability

One has to get to a state of credibility
One has to let go of all that creates immobility

To feel that state of wholesome peace
One has to learn when to let go when to release

One has to know when to act and when to cease
One has to be aware of her being piece by piece

One can't experience the light by avoiding understanding of the dark
One can't swim the whole ocean without learning to deal with the shark

One can't get to wholesome without having to sense an embark
One can't find how to remove the stain without first having a mark

Poem by Roya R. Rad

Ego Creates Distractions

It would be great if we get to the point where we realize that the world does not revolve around us, after all. It is really not that small to focus on one point of existence. Most everything we do before reaching a self-awareness phase is from that point of view, me, my, and mine. This includes pigeonholing, labeling, and taking things too personally. When someone does something we consider rude, or a disrespectful behavior, etc., we keep a sense of rancor for a long time. While the actual incident may have taken a few minutes, we preserve it for what seems like forever. We categorize, label, and stereotype unfairly, based on our conditioning, in a way that could be based on personal perceptions, not the facts. We think that because something is ours, it is making us better, but we don't take into account the fact that it is not what we hold, but what we do with what we hold. In other words, do we use the knife to perform surgery and heal someone or do we use it to rob someone of their property? The knife is not the object of value. It is what the person who holds it does with it that makes it a valuable vs. destructive tool. This can be applied to anything we hold, from what we were born with to what we have acquired throughout life. The question is, what are we doing with the means we have? Are we acting selfishly or selflessly? What evidence do we have that it is one and not the other? Once we start to examine it, we may be surprised by how wrong some of our perceptions have been.

If we start the self-reflection process and gain more knowledge of why we act the way we do, our general understanding will increase. Most of us act unreasonably negatively when we function through a defense system called projection. Projection happens when individuals deny their thoughts and emotions and throw them to the outside world. It happens when individual's unacceptable or threatening feelings are repressed, and then ascribed to someone else. It is a hidden and subtle psychological process and needs a great degree of self-knowledge to be able to access. How it works is that it helps individuals who are uninformed about their whole self by denying possession of what they don't accept. For example, a woman who has hidden intense jealousy for everything around her, but does not admit to it, may see everyone's behavior as jealous or threatening. Someone who does not feel smart enough may see everyone as stupid. Someone with a sense of inner anger may categorize others as angry. Someone with an inner sense of inferiority may categorize others as low. It is worth knowing that how individuals react to situations has more to do with their inner world than with the outer one, namely us. This will make it easier for us to let go of what is not worth carrying.

That said, let's go to the balance point and what it means in this case. Just because we learn that some people project does not mean we should exaggerate this to every situation and categorize every act we don't like as projection. This will take us into avoidance and denial. Our interactions with people teach us a great deal about ourselves and how to deal with situations. They are an important part of our life. If we put all the blame on others, it won't be much of an eye-opening experience. When we explain actions as projections, we are only referring to unreasonable and negative ones. For example, someone who is being rude to us for no reason, a friend making up harmful stories about us, a cashier throwing money at us, someone on the street giving us a bad look, a co-worker wanting to step over us, or someone acting towards us with discrimination when we didn't really do anything to trigger that kind of reaction. But a normal reaction cannot be categorized as projection. We all react to situations that seem reasonably threatening and become defensive. Again, the key is the reaction being in proportion and fair to the action. For example, if Julia's husband comes home after a full day of work and the first thing Julia does is complain about her day, taking her anger out on him, if her husband reacts with an upset voice, she shouldn't be taking it as "just another one of his projections." This does not fall into that category. This is more a reaction to Julia's action which is not that disproportionate, and has a root-oriented systematic issue that needs to be addressed.

Our ego will continuously try to tussle with us. It comes out through anxiety and fear to gain attention and control. It will do anything to take us back to the surface. It can make us feel like crying, praying, meditating, and doing anything within our power to fight it. The remedy is to recognize our higher self, put it in charge of the ego, and focus on it. Ego's limited sense of being and immaturity can bring a lot of pain and damages in life if a higher element does not interfere.

We all have our moments in which it gets challenging to restrain this ego. Ego changes shape and face. It could even come through as if it is our passion, but if we get into the pattern of self-reflection, evaluation, checking, and re checking our intentions, the process gets more transparent. Ego's intention is to satisfy the lower needs, because it is a primitive and child-like state of us. While the higher self's intention is to be in harmony with the role we came to play and to help us connect to and become an evolved soul. Some faces that the ego gives are straightforward and easy to see, but other ones are harder. It takes an advanced mind to evaluate her true intentions and that of others.

Ego may even go as far as acting a certain way to manipulate us into seeing something as a good deed or coming from the higher self, even though it's just another of the ego's basic need-satisfaction strategies. To clarify, let me use an example. Have you seen someone who says they are doing a public service, but their intent is to only get money, power, attention, or some other form of egoistic gain? It could even be an escape for them rather than truly bringing a change. I think we all have seen cases like that, if we look into it deeply. When the higher self is in charge, one may still get the attention, money, power, and anything that comes with the conquest, but those are not her main intention. Her intention is purely to create something positive and to bring out her best, because that gives her a sense of true contentment no matter what the outcome. A contented self gives more than she receives and does not take advantage. If we all get to that point, the world would be a balanced place. At times, it may get really hard to distinguish the two and see through an intention, since there are so many methods performers use to make the phony look like the real thing. As I said, it takes an evolved mind to be able to see this ego's tricks, since it does anything to make sure we can't catch her. We have all seen non-genuine egoistic imitators who attract thousands and thousands of people and make millions. We have also seen those with pure intentions doing the same. So, which is which, and how would we find out? The answer is awareness and being well-informed. A self-educated individual lessens her chances of being fooled and becoming just another mindless slave and follower.

Ego can also be tricky to deal with when one is doing self-refection. It does anything to trick us. It is worth mentioning again and again that ego is not a bad or good thing, it simply is a part of who we are. But, it is our primitive and impulsive side, a child-like side of us that needs to be guided. We have to bring out the guidance and higher side to have this ego under control. So, we are not getting into the classification of bad vs. good again. If we do that, we think we must deny or avoid ego, and that creates repression. As I mentioned earlier, what we see as separates are nothing more than extensions of one another.

So, the key is finding a way for these elements to work together like a team, rather than going against each other. Otherwise, the ego will use anything it can to take us back to the surface. It would come out in the form of unreasonable fear, worry, anxiety, and nervousness, or will make things look attractive only to manipulate our senses into thinking we need something that we really don't, or to distract us. It is a thing of the shallow and has no interest in doing the work that is needed to go to the deep. Shallow becomes its comfort zone, and anything outside of it is nothing more than a threat.

If not guided, ego can turn into this spoiled little kid who continuously fights for control. It does not want us to learn new things and expand, since that would remove attention from it. It has no interest in learning more than the basics, and its maneuver is to make us believe that we know all there is to know, and there is really nothing else to learn, or that there is no point to learning, or that learning is boring, etc. It just wants to play games and have fun at all costs. Ego needs love, discipline, and guidance, just like a child. Neglecting it will only create problems for us.

When we function from a higher self that is awake and attentive, our ego cannot deceive us anymore. We pay close attention to what matters and take no notice of what does not. We won't be a passive victim and a slave of the ego's needs and desires. We will have the power to guide the path of our life with wisdom and choice. We will become a master of our own existence, getting one step closer to our whole self and full potential as we move forward. We will be able to see reality as it is, take less than we give, feel more at peace, be content with simple things, and have more productivity. We don't waste energy on the useless and can get rid of unnecessary distractions, since we don't function out of anxious attachment but love; a love that is not defined by a certain set of non-genuine, meaningless, and repetitious behaviors, but an internal state of being. It is an innate state that resurfaces as we get rid of the contamination and start cleaning the core.

We may even get to a point where we recognize that there is no way we can evaluate the world and its participants based on external factors, images, and presentations because there are so many features behind the surface. This is where an inner sense of acceptance and being non-judgmental come to be. We may still have preferences, but it does not come from a negative place. Acceptance does not mean we accept whatever life or others toss at us. It does not mean that we are supposed to be inactive victims of life, and have no way of protecting the self and having boundaries; this is a misconception. In an ideal world, in which everyone has evolved to her full potential, there would be no need to learn skills for protecting the self, but unfortunately we are far from that at this point. There are many people who are being run over by their ego and have no real boundaries; they may want to take advantage of others to gain something. Therefore, for an evolved mind, and learning assertiveness and self-defense are important. Therefore, acceptance is not about passivity and being blind, but is about having no inner sense of resentment, anger, hate, or any negative feeling, even while one is condemning an act. With understanding and acceptance, forgiveness becomes effortless. When dealing with problems, this sense of inner acceptance can helps us come up with solutions from a more rational perspective.

Forgiveness is not a set of words or a certain way of behavior. It is an inner feeling of letting go. The foundation of forgiveness is an understanding of the fact that people are not naturally born to do evil or damaging behaviors. Everyone's essence is instinctively noble. However, the way we are raised, what we have received from the environment, predisposed genetic factors, among other reasons may make us more amenable to certain negative elements in life, which may lead us to be more susceptible to harmful acts. This understanding does not provide an excuse for the act, but an explanation. Explanation increases understanding. But there is no denying the fact that to live in a society as a group, each individual has to be held accountable for smashing other people's rights. There is always free will and a choice; the individual, at any given moment of life, can make a choice to make changes. Therefore, forgiveness is letting go of the useless inner feelings and thoughts. It is not being passive about situations. For example, it is not inviting an abusive father without having boundaries, only to let him abuse us again, but it is the ability to process and let go of the harmful memories this abusive father created.

Misconceptions about forgiveness and compassion can create confusion, so I will use another example to clarify. Let's use an individual whom we'll name Emma. Emma felt that she was emotionally abused by her husband for many years. According to Emma's explanation of the situation, her husband seemed to be a passive aggressive manipulator, creating a lot of confusion and anxiety in Emma. The examples she used supported the validity of her feelings. The goal for Emma was not to change her husband. Wanting to change others is a sense of conscious or unconscious need to control our surroundings, because we may have a lack of inner control. Emma was learning that if we don't solve problems from a root-oriented perspective, things may change on the surface, but they will come back in different shapes and forms. Consequently, she had decided to work on herself to make rational decisions as to how to deal with this situation and the anxiety she was carrying.

The goal was intervention as well as prevention. While Emma was learning to let go of any negative feelings like resentment, rage, anger, and hate toward her husband; she was finding solutions to make sure he had no way of damaging her anymore. At the end, she decided to end the relationship and worked on ways to heal the damages while letting go of any negative feelings attached to her due to her ex. Also, since they two had children, she had to have clear goals and boundaries as to how she wanted to deal with her ex, since it seemed that in some ways he had to be still a part of her life. This needed a lot of learning and implementing. She learned about her ex's condition, which by itself gave her a sense of forgiveness and compassion seeing that it is him who is really suffering the most. At the same time, she discovered ways to deal with him when she absolutely had to relate to her children's needs without being affected by his negative behavior. Once Emma learned how not to be the target of her ex's inner anger, she was free of it. He was still the same guy and since he did not seem to be interested in seeking therapy or doing any sort of self-reflection, he may never change, and may find other targets to manipulate, but Emma was not going to be one of those targets. That was all that really mattered, since Emma is not responsible for his actions and his choice of what he wants to do with his free will. But for Emma, he did not exist as this big element of her life, controlling every aspect of it. Once she made the choice to let his negativity go, he was gone. There was nothing he could do to affect her, and since he did not get the attention that a manipulator seeks, he removed his focus from Emma because she was not an easy target anymore.

Too many times we do not find ways to deal with a situation that is unfair and damaging to us. We make ourselves available to others' off-putting treatments for whatever reason, guilt, fear, insecurity, pure laziness, or lack of self-trust. We may even take a role that was created for us, the role of the victim. We start to believe this role, and our inner feelings get blemished with negativity. We get engulfed in this negativity, and it drains all our available energy and resources. Therefore, not knowing that there are more options than our stressed mind is allowing us to see, we cannot focus on finding a solution..

To end this chapter, let's ask ourselves, is it me or is it you? The answer would be that it is probably more me than I ever thought. It is usually either that we were the ones with the hurtful act (or maybe we were) or because we put our self in a position to be the target of that act. Further, it is us who make a choice of carrying the symptoms of an act for years, long after the act is literally over. I do realize that there are exceptions to every rule, and there are cases that are very complex, but it is good to know the general rule, because most of us fall into that category. It is also worth noting that we cannot expect ourselves to feel interested and attracted to everyone and everything. We may even feel more repulsed toward certain acts as we see deeper. If we have a certain path of life we are taking, there are certain preferences we will have that are in harmony with the goals of that path. To be able to focus, we need to let go of unnecessary distractions. However, it becomes questionable when we start thinking that whoever is different from us or not similar to what we present is not good enough. That is where bias and discrimination are at work. The end point is that having preferences, while at the same time having an inner feeling of acceptance, is healthy and normal.

False vs. Genuine Interaction

I am tired of an imposter smile
Making an inch look like a mile

Non-genuine words with hidden hostility
Make one wonder if the time is worthwhile

Pointless forthcoming
Talking like we are humming

The truth is right before our eyes
But we believe our own lies

Even in the daylight
We are searching for the sun's ignite

We are sitting face to face
But we don't see each other's base

We don't even look at each other
And when we do, all we see is smother

Not with ears, not with our eyes
Can we hear or see each other's cries

We seem lost in this warped world
We are looking for love, but we are swirled

Poem by Roya R. Rad

What Would All The Learning Do For Us?

You may ask, so what is the point of all this learning and developing? I would say, give me a more valuable point to live for and I will be happy to take that route. It's like asking what is the point for my child to go to school? The point is what you make the point to be. If I decide that my child should not learn, then I better have something better planned and offered. And we are all responsible for that inner child.

Learning and application of what is learned make it easier for us to be who we came here to be. Learning can teach us that things we have spent so much time separating are, in reality, complementary of each other. For example, for too long we have been trying to separate spirituality from science, while more and more we are becoming aware of the fact that if one denies the other, there is no integrity to the process. It is worth noting that when I use the words spirituality or religion, I don't mean a set of ritualistic behaviors or thinking patterns which have been copied from generation to generation without knowing why or questioning their relevance to and for the present time.

When I use the words spirituality or religion, I mean a set of deep divine beliefs that life is bigger than what is seen. I further mean implementing certain personal practices that help us with understanding our place and role in this bigger picture, and how it interacts with us. This is a personal experience that cannot be imposed. The whole concept of free will would be tarnished if one thinks that she can force a set of spiritual beliefs onto others. As evolved minds, we feel less and less of the need to follow others and more and more of the need to discover the truth, and follow our own path after that discovery. We seem to idealize others less, and see that those whom we considered super-human of some sort are human after all. What may set them apart is that they seem to have successfully accessed their core essence, their role in life, and their mature self. They seem to be in control of their ego.

In addition, when I use the word science, I mean hard core science dealing with data and facts, and I do understand that science can sometimes contradict itself, but for the serious seeker there is more than enough information to lead the way.

Learning is a process that gets deeper and moves faster as we go along. But, one needs to be careful to check for the intent behind the learning every once in a while, to make sure it is not just feeding the ego but is for having this need of understanding. In addition, it has to be complemented with practicing what is being learned.

Living in two countries, traveling to new places, and doing research, I have observed discrimination, prejudice, negative views, and racism toward other groups of people who are different from the majority, everywhere in the world. Contradictory to the general view, there seem to be more of these biased views in less advanced countries than the ones we consider to be more developed. In addition, the less mature-minded individuals with limited or no knowledge about a particular group seem to have more negative opinions about that group that are not factual in nature. I have been amazed over and over again by how much people who hardly know each other categorize and judge each other, and cannot help but wonder what this is doing to us all from a whole perspective.

We hear more stories of discrimination in the more developed countries because of two simple facts: 1. The fact that more developed countries seem to attract a variety of people, due to opportunities provided, so people are personally exposed to these differences more and have to learn new skills to deal with them. 2. The fact that developed countries usually have evolved more anti-discrimination rules and laws for human rights, and give people a voice if thoy are broken, so we tend to hear more of these types of stories. This is a good reminder that just because we hear it more at one place and not another does not mean that it exists more there. It just means that due to the nature of interactions it is heard more often, and people are becoming more aware of it.

As we move forward in life, as science is expanding and stepping more and more into the previously marked "mysteries," and as learning is more accessible and a necessity, we are starting to comprehend what many of the highly actualized and transformed individuals have been trying to communicate with us for thousands of years. They were communicating some of the same concepts, but with more simplicity and less technicality, perhaps because of the evolutionary process, and maybe they wanted to make sure that the people of their time could understand it. But, when reading through some of their messages, we can't help wondering how they knew that. They seemed so far ahead of their time, and were sometimes misunderstood. They seemed to have experienced a lot of hardship to get their message across. They were judged, sometimes harmed, and at points ridiculed for their messages. That said, we can't help asking, being so far ahead of their time, did these individuals have access to something unseen? Did they connect with something mysterious? Then we get to a point where we realize that what may seem like a mystery to us may have been just another reality for them, and ask why. Perhaps because they were able to bring out their higher self and connect to their source with an open but thirsty mind, get rid of all the heavy extra-worldly attachments, superfluous baggage, and impulsive neediness. They were able to focus and discover. They were aware of the truth of their ego, and how it wasn't their whole self. That is when they were able to get to a state of self-transparency and were able to reflect to others the information they received. What they held was pure knowledge, because information has always been there. As time goes on, we are able to access and discover it more, some of us faster than others, but all of us have the potential if we choose to use it.

As we are evolving consciously, we are learning that by cooperating, respecting differences, not trying to impose our own values and beliefs on others, and valuing others as human beings with rights, we are making it easier for ourselves to accomplish our lives' goals and move forward. As we become more aware, we realize that whatever we do, even the deepest form of behaviors, comes from a self mode. The more we realize this, the less we want to take credit for our good actions, and take responsibility for our bad actions, and become more reasonable when it comes to expectations.

I remember mentioning this in one of my seminars. A lady asked me how that would apply to a mother who would sacrifice everything for her child. How could that be categorized as something coming from a self mode?

I used an example of a mother who would throw herself at a car if the car was about to hit her child, to save the child. I went further, explaining that mother would mainly do that because the feeling of losing a child is unbearable for her to live with. It is true that it is a sacrifice, but she did it for "her" child and may not do the same for someone else's child. It was hers, and that is why she was protecting her. It was coming from a self mode. Now, this is as deep as it can get, you can go on forever with examples in which we really think we are doing something for others but it is all within a self mode. Once we learn more, we realize that this is not a bad thing, and is a normal part of the process. We simply have needs that we have to pay attention to. The higher we go, the deeper the needs.

I have asked questions from people from all walks of life about this subject. The answer always goes back to "me," but is very different whether their realization of this "me" is from a more primitive and egoistic self or a higher self. For example, we call someone who always functions from an egoistic me as an arrogant, narcissistic, and selfish person, while we deeply respect those who function from a higher kind of me. It is a totally different experience, depending on which "me" we are trying to fulfill.

We all innately have the ultimate need of becoming self-actualized, becoming authentic, and having a concrete identity that is not changed by outside factors but evolved by inside modes. Whether we are consciously aware of this or are unconscious of it does not change the fact that we have the innate need for it, and that if we ignore it, no matter what we do throughout our life, we will have a feeling of insecurity and inner anxiety. In other words, we will feel an internal sense of conflict.

The quest for spirituality, self-development, and self-growth are just some of the examples of how badly we really want it. We want to become a drop of the ocean that is holding all the characteristics of the ocean, but with a separate sense of identity. We want to become selfless, but self-knowing. This life will give us the opportunity to learn how to be what we innately crave for. But why many of us don't pursue or realize it is not because we are incapable, but because we get fixated on fulfilling the lower needs and stay in a circular pattern rather than moving up. These lower needs can start from the most basic needs like food, shelter, and sex to the next level of needs like a sense of social and individual security, to the need for having healthy relationships with others and feeling loved and respected, to the need to feel confidence in ourselves and trust our inner self. While passing and fulfilling these needs, we have the opportunity to learn and expand and get close to self-actualization. Once we become self-actualized, we can go through another level, which is that of self-transformation. Therefore, as you can see, this process is usually not something that can be accomplished quickly. It takes work, knowledge, focus, and awareness. It also takes someone who is open to the mysteries of life.

Once we get to the top level of self, we don't function based on neediness, but on the flow of a natural state of being some call pure love. Once we get there, everything we do is out of love, not need. We still have needs, basic and advanced ones, but we are in complete control of when, how, and where we want these needs met. We are not slaves but masters of our own functioning.

I used the example of the drop in the ocean. Water has been used as a metaphor for spirituality for thousands of years by many. When looking at water and its properties, it is easy to see that water has no shape of its own but takes the shape of any object that it occupies. To relate this to self-actualization and self-transformation, when a person gets to the state of self-actualization, she becomes molded into her real self. She has a shape, an identity that knows its role and qualities. Then, after this, comes another level, self-transformation. At this stage, the individual becomes selfless while fully aware of the sense of "self" she posses. So, in a way, she possesses a self, but does not "need" it anymore, since she has become selfless. At this stage, the individual becomes like pure water, a drop of the ocean, with all the characteristics of the ocean. I have talked extensively about the stages of self-growth and the pyramid of needs in my other books. It is a fascinating modality, which can help in understanding the process of life. I will elaborate in the upcoming chapter about ego and what it is.

We humans get so fixated on the shallow, and so conditioned to think that's all there is, that we forget about searching for the truth. We spend too much time categorizing, reacting to our categorization, finding ways to prove our categorization is right, and celebrating our sense of being right. We try to find fulfillment in the wrong place. Many times, what we categorize as good or bad is more like an out of balance force, like a certain type of behavior, thought, or action. For example, anger is not bad, but neither is it good by itself. It just is a part of us as humans; it is an emotion. If this emotion is acknowledged and the seed is planted naturally, then the anger, in a balanced form called assertiveness, is created. If we are aware, we are in control of this seed, know how to nurture and use it, and not the other way around. A healthy anger can be defined as assertiveness, which is a necessary tool for someone who wants to move forward in life and accomplish goals. To be able to deal with modern society, with all the expectations from one's surroundings, one has to learn to assert herself to define and defend her boundaries, and to make sure she is not stepped on. So, anger in the form of self-defense is needed, or we struggle through life feeling like the passive victims.

A passive human usually feels taken advantage of, may numb herself to not be able to feel the feeling, and may look at unjust situations and have no inner reaction. Such a person may feel like a victim, or she may not discover many things about herself because she stayed as a passive observant rather than an active participant in many situations that she could have learned from. She may not stand up for what she thinks is right and may hold a lot of inner anger and resentment, consciously or unconsciously. On the other side of the spectrum, if there is too much of the feeling of anger, it can turn into aggression. Aggression is a destructive force; it is when someone attacks another, not because of self-defense, but for other intentions like taking advantage, harming, damaging, crossing boundaries, power struggle, fulfilling egoistic needs through others, etc.

How each force is to be played is a completely personal and unique experience. There is a center to all of us. We need to discover it and work our way out from that starting point, not the other way around. So bad and good, sin and virtue, low and high, all become personal experiences, depending on the level of understanding we are at, and how close or far away we get from this center point.

A sin is whatever distances us from our center, and a good deed is whatever keeps us closer to our center. So, in a way, good and bad, or hell and heaven, have personal realities to them. All the tools, religious rules, teachings, education, etc., are just that; tools. We can use them to our benefit to learn and get closer to our center. Or we can use them as just another categorization tool and source of distraction that would make us delusively feel superior and get even further from our essence.

This essence can be called different things by different people. If you want to call it soul, you can. The point is not to get too indulged into how things are labeled but what they mean to us. Soul, essence, spirit, psych, core, and center all mean the same, coming from the same source. That invisible force used to be a complete mystery, but thanks to today's evolution in science, it is much more comprehensible now. It is the one that is unlimited but yet within reach, the one that includes the total opposite of all that there is; a true omnipresent and omnipotence.

It is time to stop separating, and learn how things complement each other. So, learning is a blessing beyond any other when balanced with applying what is learned.

Wake up call

What we need to pay attention to, we isolate from
What we need to stay away from, we have become

When we need to connect, we detach
When we need to let go, we try to catch

What we need to use, we put aside
What we need to get rid of, becomes our pride

Distractions turn into attractions
Mind illnesses create group reactions

We want to feel right, we don't know how
We try to connect, we don't allow

We talk the talk, but there is no true walk
We take a few steps toward the mistaken block

We keep our mind on a misguiding source
We cannot learn the truth from an untrue course

We neglect the unseen force
We feel a sense of remorse

When does it stop, when does it end?
All of that is in your hand, my friend

Poem by Roya R. Rad

How To Distinguish The Ego From The Higher Self?

Hopefully, by now we know that we humans are multifaceted and are made of many layers. It starts with the most dense and physical coating, going to the most transparent ones. How one goes about naming these different layers is not the point here, but how one understands their functionality is the focus of this chapter. Again, we don't want to get too indulged in terminology, but in application.

We are physical, emotional, mental, intellectual, and spiritual beings. If we acknowledge one but not the other, we are hindering the harmonizing process between these elements and blocking the concept of full potential. Imagine our body; if our legs grow but not our hands, our body will be classified as disproportionate by a physician. The same goes for the deeper stuff we are made of. All our elements should be growing in harmony. For example, if we are too intellectual, but do not know how to handle and respond to our emotions, we have work to do.

Now let's go to the concept of ego and where its place is. There are many modalities that give slightly different terminology to the human psyche and the position of ego. But in the end, they complement each other. For this chapter, we will explain Carl Jung's terminology. In general, a human's psyche is made up of the ego, the conscious, unconscious, and collective unconscious. I have talked about Carl Jung in my other books and will do even more in my upcoming book which will compare Carl Jung's concepts with that of Maslow's on a human's sense of self. But to give relevant basic information, the ego is the more primitive side of us, but primitive does not mean bad. Primitive just means that it should not be sitting in the driver seat. If it does, there will either be no real destination, or a disaster is going to happen. Saying that ego is a bad thing is like telling a first grader that she is bad because she is not at a higher grade level. This means that we are neglecting the fact that a first grader simply cannot be at a higher level until she finishes one grade level at a time. If she is pushed and skips a couple of grades and jumps to something she is not ready for, she will not be capable of understanding what is being taught. Therefore, the ego, which is a normal part of all, of us needs to be attended to, nurtured, disciplined, and be taken over by a higher side of us.

We can call this ego the child self, the primitive self, the immature self, or the lower self. How we feel comfortable naming it is not the point. What matters is that ego is a part of us and we cannot deny, avoid, or try to belittle it; and we certainly cannot let it be in charge, representing itself as our whole self. As we grow older, our other sides, like the adult part or the guidance part, should come out and take charge of the ego. If we let the ego be in charge, we may be drawn to the shallow and the unimportant, since the ego is only attracted to childish stuff and cannot comprehend, nor can it see, the deep. It relies on the five senses to classify something as existing. Its intent is to play and have childish fun, and could not care less about learning or growing. It is simple; it cannot care for something that it does not understand. It cannot comprehend that there are consequences for decisions and actions in life. Its focus is on instant gratification and satisfying desires, without paying attention to short- or long-term cost. It has no concept of delaying gratification and waiting to evaluate situations, since it is not mature enough to do so. If it is not disciplined and taken control of, it becomes a spoiled child where all she wants is take, take, and take, without ever feeling satisfied or fulfilled. The more it gets, the more it wants. Just like a child, it needs an adult's guidance to learn how to act. The adult system should have a clear boundary with this ego. That adult guidance is a built-in system within our package of self, and is within all of us. The more we focus on it and its growth, the better we can benefit from it and hear it's signals.

To clarify this point, there is absolutely nothing wrong with having some moderate amount of childish fun and pleasure in life, but it has to be supervised by our adult or guidance sides. We cannot let our ego make decisions for us. For example, when we go to college, our main intent is to graduate, and hopefully learn, but it has been shown that the happier we are, the more our brain can learn. So, things that give us some sort of having fun and feeling happy are necessary to increase productivity and openness to learning. It would be hard for a person who is depressed or sad to learn as much. The same is true with other parts of life. We all want to feel some form of joy and happiness, but when we let our ego be in charge, these concepts become very confusing to us. The way we define happiness is not what truly makes us happy. We keep on chasing it, but never feel like we really have it. We may experience momentary states of happiness by using any external factor we can get our hands on, and usually we have to pay a high price for that short happiness. In other words, the cost outweighs the benefit. To truly feel content, joyful, and to be able to find pleasure from simple things in life, we don't need to go far, if we learn to take charge of what is within.

Ego has many shapes and forms. It may come in the form of unreasonable fear, a sense of unreasonable obligation, or guilt, all of which can create resentment and anger. Ego's feelings, thoughts, and behavior are immature. At the end, the uncontrolled ego's characteristics are those of an undeveloped, unreasonable, and impulsive person.

So, we can ask ourselves these questions to see where our intentions lie:

1. Is it coming from our ego or a higher state?
2. Am I carrying a baggage of anxiety, fear, anger, resentment, jealously, or any other negative emotions, passively or actively, consciously, or unconsciously?
3. Am I continuously behaving in a way to get attention, even if this behavior is not adding to my growth in any way?
4. Do I have a nonstop need for instant gratification? Do I think of the consequences of my behavior, thoughts, and emotions? If so, how far can I think of these consequences, short term or long term?
5. How deeply can I see through these consequences?
6. Do I continuously find myself being upset by my surroundings, and for my inability to accept it without putting any effort into changing what does not work for me?
7. Do I feel like life is resisting me and there is nothing I can do?
8. Can I calm myself down before acting?
9. Am I impulsive? Am I in control of me?
10. Do I find myself consciously being affected by the outside world, being dragged from one edge to the other, being affected by other people's acts, advertisements, and what others think, without evaluating their validity? Or am I immune the mind's diseases that are out there?
11. Do I feel like I am just a passive follower who wants

to belong, or am I an active participant who learns and experiences?

12. Do I have values, and, if so, what are they based on and what steps am I taking to follow my own values? Are my values just a series of meaningless ritualistic repetitions, or did I spend a lot of time and effort evaluating and setting my life's values?
13. Are my values my own, or do I mimic them from someone else without knowing why they are beneficial to my core?
14. When I evaluate my life, have I made improvements? Do I feel like I am moving forward?
15. Do I know what my role is in this life, and am I content with myself, or do I keep on wanting to be others?
16. Am I just sucking out of life or am I contributing to it?
17. If there was no one around and no one was listening, what would I say would be my real intention behind my behaviors and the way I live?
18. Am I willing to do anything, even if it goes against my values, to get fame, money, and my basic needs met?
19. Do I feel like I am chasing my own tail and not really moving forward in life?
20. Is it easy for me to be manipulated by what I see, hear, etc., or do I have the ability to think things through to see whether they are right, based on factual evidence?
21. Am I interested in learning new things every day?

22. Do I have limited information about things and become judgmental toward them?
23. Am I selective and conscious of what I invite to my life, or do I have to deal with too many unnecessary distractions?

These are questions that can be helpful in the self-reflection process. When it comes to the higher self, there are many levels to it. The more evolved one's psyche and mind get, the more one is able to access this higher self. This holds on to an adult side, a parent side, and a guidance side. So, if we don't think we had a perfect childhood with parents or role models who disciplined us right or loved us enough, here is our chance to bring out the parent and guide in us and fill the gap. This can be a good resource for us to overcome any potential excuses and move toward possibilities. The higher self is the one that uses rational and logical decisions, considers and evaluates ones emotions and thoughts, and takes into account the short and long-term consequences of these decisions. It feels the most intense feelings, but does not get engulfed in them and does not drag them; it gets the signal and moves on. It also helps the individual see more into the bigger picture than from a limited personal viewpoint.

These are just some of the questions we can ask ourselves to see if the more mature side of us is in control:

1. Do I have clear self-affirmed goals for my life that match my capabilities, and that are based on my needs and potential?
2. Am I overestimating or underestimating myself, and do I have evidence to support this?
3. Do I look at facts behind information, or do I impulsively follow others without knowing whether they are right?
4. Am I a follower, or do I have my own set of clearly chosen values?

5. Are my behaviors and my lifestyle mostly in accord with my values?
6. Does my lifestyle match my objectives in life?
7. Do I act impulsively in most strains of my life, or can I delay a decision to think it through, based on factual information?
8. Can I stand up to what I believe, even if I feel like it may cost me time, effort, and rejection? Or do I act as if I agree with others even though I really don't? If so, why is that?
9. Can I manage my thought, emotions, and behaviors most of the time, or do I spend a lot of time undoing damages I create for myself?
10. Can I stop an irrational thought when it comes to my mind?
11. Do I have a delayed reaction time to a thought in which I can do the cost/benefit analysis?
12. Am I good with time management and my boundaries?
13. Am I aware of my limitations? If so, am I finding ways to work on them?
14. Am I learning something new and valid every day about myself and my environment?

To end this chapter, if we want to find the whole self, we need to bring out the guidance and parent self, give the child self love and discipline and bring all these elements together to work in harmony rather than going against each other. We have to find a middle ground to unite them and help them merge. The only reason that they may go against each other is our self-neglect, which would create negativity, unproductively, and wastefulness. The more we bring these parts of our self to work together, the closer we get to our whole self, and the less energy we spend focusing on primitive needs. As our guidance and adult sides come to take charge, we become more mature and focused. We also need to give ourselves necessary attention for growth, give ourselves rewards, be careful not to push ourselves too hard, be a kind to ourselves, and enjoy the fruits of our work. Only then we can project what we have achieved onto others. Our mature sides can help us bring nurturing into our relationships, speaking with genuine love, performing kind acts, practicing giving, and giving others honest compliments. We learn to show an extra consideration to others, since we are really showing it to ourselves. What we give, and the intention with which we give it, will be reflected back to us, and that is nurturing to our essence. We need to look closely at our intentions. The deeper we get, the more transparent this intention will be.

Inner Freedom

Freedom is a special inner concession
We can have access by self-confession

When the door of wakefulness unlocks
When we get rid of any sort of blocks

Something pours, some form of a drift
As if we let go of a long time heavy lift

We feel lighter and lighter
The outlook looks brighter

Our vision becomes more clear
As we learn to release our fear

Fear of rejection, fear of isolation
Turn into a complete sense of admiration

We get to a center place in creation
Where there is no sense of frustration

It is were we belong, there is no temptation
All that is, is a feeling of dedication

It is where we glance from the above
That we know what it means to feel love

The love was with us all along
We were just distracted for too long

Poem by Roya R. Rad

How To Self-Reflect Instead Of Self-Neglect?

Self-doubt is a block to moving forward and growing. With all the mind diseases that are around, and all the people who are trying to tell us what to do, how to think, how to be, if we can't think for ourselves and are not aware, we go further and further away from our true sense of being. If we lack an inner sense of confidence, and if we doubt our own truth, it will be easy to be manipulated. If we doubt ourselves, we neglect paying attention to our essence.

The farther away we get from our truth, the more confusing it gets. We are puzzled by why we feel the way we do. In some cases, we may even have achieved materialistic senses of life, but still feel unsatisfied. There is something missing. But what is it? We have been chasing other people's beliefs, dreams, ideas, and rules of life rather than that of our own. What a feeling of loss if we suddenly become aware! But we have to realize that it is never too late. Self-doubt is created when we want to imitate others and want to have what others possess, thinking that it is what we need, and want to copy other people's ways of thinking. As soon as we start challenging those patterns and pay attention to our essence, we are on our way to building an inner confidence.

When we doubt ourselves, we forget about our individuality, uniqueness, and our place in the world. We don't have boundaries, we feel stepped over, taken advantage of, and overwhelmed. Too many of us are spending too much time undoing the damages others created, due to lack of clear boundaries. This is the energy and time we could have spent building something.

Self-doubt comes when we don't know who we are. When we trust others' opinions and thoughts more than we trust ourselves; when we don't think we are good enough to have self-value, to have needs, to have ideas based on facts and knowledge, and to want to grow. Self-doubt causes us to escape from ourselves and continually focus on others, satisfying others consciously or unconsciously, a service that will only create resentment and anger rather than love and connection. It creates negativity because it is not based on love but is rooted in a sense of escape; an escape from self. When we provide service to others from a state of self-knowledge and awareness, we do it from a place of purity. Therefore, it does not create any resentment or negative feeling. Instead, it creates a sense of inner joy, love, and connection. Nothing good can be created if the seed is anxiety, escape from the self, fear, and a lack of awareness. At the end, self-doubt opens the door to self-neglect.

The question of how to self-reflect instead of self-neglect can be a tricky one. Most of us think that to care for our self just means to care for the physical body, or doing things like getting a message, going to a retreat, doing something fun, going shopping, talking to someone, exercising, taking care of physical health etc. While there is no denying that doing these activities, in moderation, are important, we still need more. These are good tools to help us get physically active and healthy, calm ourselves down, enjoy life, remove attention from something that is disabling us, and relaxing and getting to that silent place, away from chaos, to recharge. But along with that there should be a time to learn about one's self and surroundings, and to practice what is being learned.

Then there is another category of self-neglect definers who think that not neglecting the self means becoming selfish. These two are complete opposites. If we neglect our self, we will become selfish, because we are being ruled by the ego up to a point where all control is within the ego's hand and we just take, take, and take from whoever crosses our path or from whatever we can get from life without spending a second thinking how we want to return the favor. In such a case, we may even give ourselves the right to move up the ladder of success, not because we truly deserve it, but because we have learned ways to manipulate or step on others. We will do anything to get our primitive needs met, even at others' expense. We think we deserve everything good we have, and everything bad we have is someone else's fault. Such a person is completely neglecting her higher self, and is living a life of internal turmoil and confusion.

Then there is yet another group, similar to the second one, who think becoming selfless means being self-neglectful, not knowing that the two are not the same at all. If we neglect our selves, it will be unlikely that we will know how to be selfless. One has to learn to pay attention to her whole being to be able to become self-aware. Such a person is able to move forward with accomplishing other steps. How do we know whether the steps we are taking are right, or whether we are acting from a selfless state of being, if we don't know who we are? Remember the mind trick It can make something look like what it is not if we lack self-awareness and are uninformed. Knowing who we are is not something we can just get; we have to have certain privileges to access it. We need to do the work. Until then, we may just hear what it means to be selfless from someone else. We may categorize ourselves as selfless and surround ourselves with those who support that view, but in the end, if we are not increasing our knowledge and practicing what we know, and if we are closing our eyes, we will lose the battle. Once we close our eyes, we see only darkness. Once we see darkness, everything that comes to us is not what it seems.

Now, that being said, we all need to recharge every once in a while. We need to be able to enjoy life and feel joy. Both learning and finding joy are part of the same process; one feeds the other. The more we learn, the more we can find joy from simpler things and the more content we become. And the more we feel joy, the easier it gets to learn. After we are able to recharge and get back to a neutral or joyful state, it is learning time again; another one of the chicken and egg episodes in which they feed each other.

After, and perhaps during, the recharging comes self-reflection. Self-reflection in the midst of emotional commotion is difficult and usually biased. One has to find a quiet inner zone to start reflecting. Now, the bad news is that self-reflection is not a set of instructions that can be given to us to follow. It is a personal practice, and depends on our type of personality, mental and emotional states, and what stage of the self-growth process we are in. One method may work for one person and not for another. We can be creative about what works for us, but until we get there we can use what has worked for others to test it. That said, there are general guidelines that can be followed. After reading these guidelines, we have to listen to our own center and see what it is that we're seeking. At the end, we have to go one step at a time and stay at a reasonable pace. There is no competition here.

Here are some of the guidelines:

1. Start with learning to be in control of your thoughts, and quieting them, or replacing them with something productive and positive. Choose a time of the day in which you can work on stopping unwanted or irrational thoughts. Start small and add to it every day. You can start with a 10 minute time-frame in the morning, noon, and evening. Focus on a thought and try to take control of it until it vanishes. Take deep breaths. It would be good if you get to a

point where you automatically can stop damaging, negative, or irrational thoughts. Remember, the human brain processes thousands of thoughts every day. Highly trained individuals can get rid of negative or unproductive thoughts quickly.

2. Learn to have boundaries for your needs, wants, desires, and sense of enjoyment. Try to focus more on simple things and learn to take pleasure doing them. If you cook, see how you can focus on cooking and make it into a fun activity; if you garden, make it pleasurable. Train your brain to enjoy what is healthy, straightforward, and in accord with your life's overall intent. Try not to waste energy on what does not matter that much, as much as possible. This way you can reduce distractions and will be able to focus on what is important. This way you won't take things that matter for granted. Having too many choices can be overwhelming to our senses. If we are constantly being asked to make a choice, we can feel drained. We find ourselves investing too much time and energy in things we have no real use for. It can create confusion and self-doubt, and even anxiety or stress. We may feel like having too many choices is becoming more weakening than strengthening. When we focus on too many things, we miss out on what is really important in our life. We have to learn to filter, and value quality rather than quantity.

3. Do self-reflection practices at least three times a day until it becomes a daily routine. You can also incorporate this self-reflection with step one. When a situation is bothering you, self-reflection can help you see rationally how you contributed to it. That, by itself, can help you plan the change. It can also help you become more aware of your emotional signals.

Question yourself to see whether there are any out of balance emotions, thoughts or behaviors that you carry, how they are affecting your life, and how you can balance them.

4. Test yourself to see how you can shift your focus onto the solution rather than the problem and how you can calm your mind.
5. Spend some time every day to learn something new. A little into a new culture, history, language, science, disease, health, disorder, condition etc; or learn something about someone, and definitely about yourself. Every day, stretch it a little farther. You will be surprised by how much you will develop by just doing this one thing. You can focus on what you judge most and learn about that first. See how factual information about something can affect your level of judgment. For example, if you judge someone due to an external factor, or if you have had access to one-sided information about something, it is a good signal for you to learn about it.
6. Evaluate your traditional values and beliefs to see whether they are helping you develop, or if they are limiting you and blocking you from growth. If the second, perhaps it is time to reconsider.
7. If you belong to any group or organization that wants to make you think you are in some way superior to others because you belong to that group, or that their way is the best and only way, you may want to see why you were attracted to that group and question your intentions.
8. In your quest for spirituality, question your intentions, since the intention is the number one key to knowing which level of spirituality you stand at. Do you want

to be spiritual out of habit, tradition, fear, escape, or a need to belong and feel important? Or is your thirst for spirituality based on a true form of love-based craving for connecting to your source?

9. Take good care of your body, eat healthily, exercise, and be selective of what you put in your body, including what type of music you listen to, what you look at and what you get from looking at it, what you smell, and what you touch. What goes in must be nurturing you and enable you to be healthy. Be selective and focus more and more on quality, not quantity. Quantity is the thing of an ego; quality is what the higher self is interested in. Stay way from chemicals, processed food, artificial flavors, alcohol, and drugs as much as possible. The more natural the food, the more harmony it has with your body. Put love and effort into preparing your food, and eat it with calm and at certain times, so your body knows what to expect from you.

10. Don't get ensnared by what is popular, but seek what is right. Be an active part of your choices, not a passive follower. Be a free soul, not a slave of external factors. At the same time, be aware.

11. Remember that no matter what baggage you are carrying, there is an essence within you that is pure and ready to move forward. After you work through your baggage, you can reach the essence and start moving. You always have the choice, and it is never too late.

12. Your expectations of yourself and your life should be reasonable, depending on your abilities, the size and weight of the baggage you're carrying, your environment, and your limitations. You should not compare your progress with another. You can only

compare it with yourself, to see how far you have gone within a certain period of time. Everyone is different, and what you see may not be what there really is, so comparison could be misleading and unfair.

13. Let your emotions come as they are. Don't push them away. If you have too much of an intense emotion that is making you feel uncomfortable, don't deny or try to avoid it. Instead, feel it and see why you are feeling the way you do. Read the signals; they have a message. If you keep avoiding your emotions, they keep coming back, repeating themselves and resurfacing, more and more intense, in the hope that they will catch your attention. However, if you learn to pay attention and experience your emotions, you can go to the root and make the needed changes, and calm them down. With this, you may benefit from professional help to support you.

14. Leave your past difficulties for a set time in which you want to analyze, process, and sort through them. Once you start this process, do not keep carrying them with you every hour of every day. There is a time and place for everything. Keep them in a closed box and open it only when you're ready to deal with them. Imagine it to be like any other part of your life. Set aside a certain time for it, and re-visit it during that time. This can be done in a counselor's office, with a trusted friend who is knowledgeable, related to the subject of self-growth, and is unbiased, or you can do it on your own if you think you are strong enough to handle it. In the end, it is your personal choice and you have to be ready for it. The point is that once you start facing and working on the repressed memories of the past, you may feel lighter. You are freeing a part of you from jail, which will give you a sense of

self-liberation. You are not escaping anymore. You are facing and moving forward.

15. Evaluate our defenses. See which ones you use more, and why you use what you use. In addition, evaluate how you can modify these defenses. At the end of this book, I have added a list of defenses.

16. Spend time every day to connect with nature and the bigger picture, whether you walk out, read a book about nature, or look at pictures. It does not matter what you do, but pay attention when you do it. Look at the smallest to the biggest things, and see how they are so very magnificent. See yourself in this unlimited picture, and see how insignificant, but at the same time priceless, you are. See how they sound like opposites, but are both a part of you. Imagine yourself as a part of this magnificent existence. Only a drop in the ocean, but a drop that is privileged to be given the free will to have all qualities of the ocean.

17. Find healthy and productive ways to interact with others, with a focus on quality (who) not quantity (how many).

18. There is something about you that is unique. Discover it.

19. Every morning when you wake up, start your day with a self-talk practice that includes certain moves, certain thoughts, and certain words that work for you. These three should be in harmony with one another. Focus on words of appreciation for your blessings, promising yourself to start your day with the intention of having your higher self in charge, admiring the beauty of nature and the universe, showing gratitude for being a part of this amazing beauty, asking forgiveness for your mistakes and taking things for

granted; using words like kindness, compassion, forgiveness, balance, focus, determination, guidance, omnipresent, whole, with pure and authentic intent. This will help start your day positive and focused. Some may prefer to repeat this at mid-day and in the evening as well, or even combine it, later on, with their self-reflection exercise. Reasonable and positive self-affirmation is also a helpful tool.

20. Work toward discovering your wholeness. That means the light, the shadow, and in between. The more you discover, the more you develop. Denial is your ego's work, and it is you worst enemy.
21. Think about the fact that you have one body and one life. With every breath you take, you are one step closer to your end of this life. So get to work.
22. Ask why, analyze, investigate, and question.
23. Check and re check your intentions and motives.

The essence

I crave your splendid present
Being with you feels so pleasant

Not knowing you, I experienced torment
Bonding with you, I sense content

As I learn to listen
I can feel myself glisten

As I learn to see
I can feel free

As I learn to feel
I find the need to reveal

As I learn to think
I focus on the synch

As I learn to become
I feel alive rather than be numb

As I learn to flow
I crave to know

I don't settle for what is below
I long for a sense of grow

Poem by Roya R. Rad

Are We Moving Backward Or Forward?

While there is no question that technologically and intellectually we are moving forward, sometimes we cannot help but wonder whether, in some aspects, we are going back to the Stone Age, where all human needs revolved around providing food and shelter. It's getting bigger, but is it getting better? It seems like the size is getting bigger, but the quality has not changed. So it makes us wonder, with this amazing technology we have access to and all the information available, with all of today's resources, why does it seem like we are stuck, and at points going backward with our self-growth process? Why do many of us work so hard to hide the truth? It seems like many of us are maturing intellectually, but not so much in other areas. Why are many of us so needy and egoistic? Why do many of us consume unreasonably without looking at the consequences from a deeper perspective? Why do many of us look at everything from a selfish viewpoint (my car, my house, my family, my job, my country, my culture, my religion, my race …) wanting to hold on to these at the cost of stepping on others, not thinking that, if we pay attention, there is really enough for all of us? Why do we destroy to gain some form of power or attention? Why do we fight so hard trying to prove what we hold is more valuable, or that we are more powerful, or that our path is the right path and that of others is wrong? Why do we want to impose our beliefs on others? Why do many of us create hostility, resentment, and anger, some consciously and some unconsciously, because of these selfish acts; and, worst of all, do it in the name of integrity?

We may have all the resources in the world, but if we don't pay attention, we won't get much out of it. We may have more, but we won't feel anything being added. If we ignore our deepest innate need, the need for self awareness, actualization, and transformation, we will make it hard for us to feel content. We feel the signals, but we ignore them. We crave something deeper, but we replace it with something meaningless. We keep on repeating the same things until we burn out without experiencing what the deep holds for us. Self-discovery is an element of life that is at the root of the problems created by us, for us, and around us.

To get more into self-discovery, when I was in my late 20s, I went through the traditional route of searching for my soul. I went to various groups to find answers. I came to notice that traditional beliefs, both Eastern and Western, were not satisfying my need. I wasn't sure what my need was, but knew that my search was not being productive the way I wanted it to be. Puzzled by the process, and having children at the same time, which opened a new door of experience to me, I went to study psychology to learn how the mind and its contents work. After that, going through a major life transition, I started to passionately analyze my life's building blocks, including its problems, and self-reflect. I became my own psychoanalyst, in a way. It was at the same time that I experienced a great deal of stress and pain, which brought self-awareness. I also started to become more and more aware of the macro picture rather than the micro. I went to explore all areas of my mind, dark and light, and learned more and more about how they can function. I was learning more and more about who I really was. The more I learned, the more I felt in charge of myself. Self-discipline was getting easier through self-awareness. I started to learn more about basics of science, physics, quantum physics, biology, chemistry, and how all of them can relate to us as human beings and our position in the universe. It gave me a good perspective to see the design and comprehend it better. As I learned more, my spiritual thirst started to become more and more satisfied, up to a point where I became spiritually comfortable. In the meantime, I started reading spiritual books and some of the spiritual methods that I thought would be helpful to me. By then they were making more sense. The more I self-reflected, the more I started to discover new dimensions of myself. I am in no way claiming that I have mastered everything. That is far from the truth. I do however, know that I am aware of myself and my surroundings more so now than ever. I also feel closer to my center. Now, this is something that we all can do. It is just a matter of readiness, or sometimes just that wake-up call.

There are many ways to word the growth process. We might call it getting deeper, more expanded, more advanced, more spiritual, or more evolved. At the end, they are all the same as far as we are finding a middle ground for learning and enjoyment, and helping them go hand in hand rather than focusing on one and ignoring the other. We have to train our mind to find a balance point between the two and help them feed each other, like a flawless system in which all forces work in harmony and cooperation. The first move toward such a system is becoming aware of what it is that is preventing us from getting there, and finding the source of the problem. Is it a certain pattern of thinking, emotion, feeling, or behavior that we keep on repeating that has become our curse? If we are fortunate enough, we will be able to discover such a pattern. If not, we will stay in the problem, being taken over by it. Then, just when we think it is at its worst, denial steps in and makes it even harder to admit to the truth. The longer we stay in denial, the deeper we get into it. We will do anything that helps us stay there, and not feel threatened, and we spend time and effort figuring out ways to stay in denial.

We become the master of manipulating our own mind. We fall sleep, we close our eyes to what life beholds, we miss out, and we feel, live, and depart empty.

Awareness is a blessing that can bring about significant inner change. It wakes us up. As we become more aware, we start noticing that everything we do either plants a new seed or nourishes a seed already in place. We are like gardeners of both light and darkness, and it is a matter of choice and knowledge to be able to plant or nourish the right seed. If we want the seed to fully grow into something beautiful, we have to plant it in the right way, time, place, and under the right conditions. There are formulas and rules for such things to work, and we cannot ignore them. We can't take no notice of rules and expect good results. If we do, we should prepare ourselves for the consequences, take them with integrity, and be accountable. At the end, if we lean something from it, we may not regret it as much. But overall, we are much better off trying not to plant any seed until we are ready for it, understand the process, and are willing to do the work.

So it is good to ask ourselves what seeds we are planting in our daily life. Are we selective about which seeds to pick and how to nourish them? If so, then we are increasing our chances of having the right fruit. Or, on the other hand, are we walking through life being totally unaware of our presence and what we are generating?

Related to planting a seed, let me give you some examples that may not be as obvious to the naked eye. For example, when one acts passively toward an abuser despite having other options, she is feeding the abuser's abusive behavior. In addition, she is feeding the passive side of herself, believing that she is a victim, or may be creating an inner sense of resentment and anger. Another example would be when we stand up for something we objectively know is just and fair, even if the majority don't think so or don't care, we are planting a seed of courage and honor in ourselves, and maybe even planting a seed of change into that situation. We may not live long enough to see that seed turn into a full-grown flower, but we would know we did something positive. Yet another example is an emotionally abusive parent who makes the child feel guilty. If such a child, as an adult, responds positively to that behavior, she is not doing anyone a service, but is feeding the negative behavior in the abuser, along with unreasonable fear and guilt in herself. Sometimes the best thing we can do for someone is to oppose them if we think they are taking the wrong road, and that could be the best support. They may not see it at the time, but again, if we are approaching the situation objectively we will have a sense of reassurance that we are doing the right thing. For many of us, standing up could be hard. Being passive may be an easy way out, an inactive passage through life, but there are times in life that we just have to move out of the comfort zone and take responsible risks. At the end, we each need to go with our own unique and individual sense of being and see what works for us.

What we don't want to do is duplicate our life's blueprint from others. We may want to look at others with an objective and open eye and learn from them, both what works and what does not, but we don't want to just pick up what they do or say without knowing why or how it would apply to us.

In the beginning of the human evolution process, imitation seemed to be the only option for survival as a group. Later on, more developed minds started to individuate, but were not always received well by their people. At times, they may have been ridiculed, or even tortured. However, at this point of time, healthy differences, creativity, and individuality seem to be cherished and celebrated more and more by our continuously advanced mind.

That being said, what we want to do is learn from those who have something valuable to offer, and see if and how it may apply to us. The point worth repeating is that we don't have to be a follower to be able to get to our wholeness. We have to learn to become objective, and have confidence enough to feel at ease with our own path. Sure, this takes a lot of time and focus, but can you name anything else that is more important?

We should not force ourselves too hard to chase something that does not make sense, seems unreal, or seems too far away. That can create confusion, and would not serve us well. We must learn to take one step at a time.

Discord

Disregarding cultures
Creates vultures

Overlooking history
Will bring about more mystery

Dispensing a nation
Is not a design of creation

Freedom is everyone's right
It doesn't know black or white

It is a personal choice
We all need to have a voice

We need to feel respected
We need to be protected

Oppression puts a stop to expression
If we can't express, forces create aggression

Aggression generates an obsession
Obsession turns into oppression

A sequence is formed
A cycle that is stormed

Who is to blame?
Who is to feel shame?

Who is the victim?
Who is the dictum?

Is the beginning an egg or a chicken?
We go on thinking until we feel sicken.

We imagine a world
Everything transformed

There is enough for all
We can keep on passing the ball

Enough is enough
No more bluff

Tell us your intention
Maybe we can plan an intervention

Poem by Roya R. Rad

For Those Of Us Thinkers, Can We Scientifically Become Spiritual?

Let's look at the word spirituality.

What does it mean?

There are many people who claim this title. I have seen people from all walks of life reporting that they are spiritual. I have seen people whose lives were great examples of true spirituality reporting that they were atheist. On the other hand, I have seen drug addicts saying they have "spiritual" feelings while using drugs. So, what does this word mean, and why such a mixed message?

The reality is that the word spirituality, or the concept of being spiritual, is not clearly understood by many people. Spirituality is not just a belief we hold, but practices we put in place to help us be more focused, fruitful, and aware in the process of life. According to Maslow, a psychologist with many years of personal and professional research, a true spirituality means a sense of self-transformation, and it can only be accomplished after a person reaches self-actualization. He further reports that only about 2%

of the population gets to be self-actualized. So, if that is the case, the percentage is even lower for highly spiritual people, the ones who are self-transformed. I have talked extensively about self-actualization in my other books, a part of which is repeated at the end of this book for your reference, but the point here is that many of us who think we are spiritual may be far away from reaching to a true sense of what it may mean for us.

So how would we know, and what does it take to be considered spiritual? The word spiritual means sacred, holy, devout, divine, and unworldly, among others. It means believing in something bigger in life, looking for the deeper truth, being devoted to one's essence, and not being attached to the material world based on a sense of neediness. Therefore, it is easy to see that just believing does not make someone spiritual. There are laws and rules that have to be followed, which needs practice. We cannot claim spirituality because we have gone to a couple of seminars here and there, go to Yoga or meditation class, go to church every Sunday, visit our Mosque every so often, or have read certain books. These can be positive steps, if taken in the right way, with the right intentions and the right provider, but the real work is the practical part of it, applying what is being learned and taking steps to start the self-discipline, self-reflection, self-awareness, and self-actualization processes.

I once interviewed a gentleman for research I was doing. This gentleman was in jail for a series of criminal activities for a long period of time. During our interview, he said that many people don't know this about him, but he has always been very spiritual, and asked me what I thought about that. When someone asks me a question, I usually answer depending on the individual's level of receptivity. In this case, the best approach for this gentleman seemed to be the direct approach, perhaps helping him break the boundless ego that had ruined his life and the lives of others. I told him he night have had spiritual beliefs, but I wasn't sure how objective those beliefs would have been. One thing seems clear, and that is that he probably was not practicing spirituality, or he would not be there. This is just another example of how people label themselves as spiritual to get a sense of inner satisfaction, while they may not know exactly what that means.

I will again touch on some of my personal experience to get to a point relevant to this chapter. Growing up as a teenager, there were a lot of changes in my childhood environment that brought about anxiety. There was economic instability, there was a revolution right when I was at a critical young age, and the revolution brought about many unexpected ups and downs to families. Then, not too long after, there was a war between Iraq and Iran which traumatized most people. Even though my city was one the ones least affected by it, no one could live out of the war zone. It was everywhere, all over the news, on the walls, pictures of people who died. Some nights we would wake up to the sound of alarms warning us to go to the basement because there was the possibility of a bomb coming toward us. These memories were the type that I repressed for a long time, not knowing that all of them were very well within me, creating inner anxiety. Back then, I started to have a deep sense of spirituality which I did not attend to. Looking back, I see that some of the sense of spirituality I was carrying was an escape rather than an inner thirst. It was more of a search for a pain reliever than a true thirst for learning. This is what I see in a lot of people. Their spirituality comes out the need to escape a painful reality. For me, it was an escape from an unstable environment. It was immature, but I thought I was extremely spiritual, even more then than now, telling me another interesting fact. The less we are spiritual, the more we may think we are.

Looking deep into my personality, some of my traits seem to have always been within me, as if I was predisposed to them, genetically and beyond. It may have taken me a while to discover what I had and help it grow. For example, a thirst and love for writing. I remember writing as early as my elementary years. During my childhood, and in my family, grades and education were highly regarded and were the most important thing. As a result, I was expected not to "waste" time on writing while I should be studying and making good grades. Later on, I forgot I had this love. I had repressed it, because I still was holding on to the view that I should not be "wasting" my time and should be making good grades and finishing my education. Not once did I start to challenge this irrational pattern of thinking that had been planted within me since childhood, even as an adult. I was bothered by the repression. It was as if something was pushing to be unleashed, but I wasn't sure what was missing. In some ways, I struggled with moving up the ladder of success in my life. I managed to do so, and finished my education as high as I could take it. It wasn't until I started the self-reflection process that I found out that the internal conflict was nothing more than a signal from within me asking me to pay attention. So, I did. Meditating, learning, reflecting, thinking, reading, and applying were the cures for me. That was and has been a rewarding process and a never-ending one.

One of the things that keeps us from discovering our spiritual self is self-doubt. Self-doubt is our number one enemy, and thanks to denial, we may not even realize we have it. Self-doubt blocks us from seeing that we are worthy of accomplishing greatness, healing, educating, creating beauty, helping others, and bringing understanding and knowledge. It prevents us from understanding that we are so much more than we see, and that we should not be wasted. Self-doubt shatters our vision from seeing that there is a deeper truth to what is on the surface. It fools us into believing that others are better than us for some external factors they have. We continuously compare our weakness with other people's false image and what they present to us, which is sometimes far from their wholeness.

Self-doubt is like an epidemic disease. It separates us into multiple characters, creating conflict, while one part of us knows we have something good to offer, the other part wants to stay in the comfort zone of denial and doubt. It does not let us see what we are capable of, preventing us from taking a risk to step out of our comfort zone and see what else is out there.

We may forget the fact that to have anything worth having takes effort, determination, and responsible risks. The more worthy, the more all those elements are needed. This inner conflict can create anxiety, stress, and other kinds of pain and negative emotions. We want to find a way to escape the pain, only to add more weight to our already heavy burden. This escape becomes a part of us, running away from a problem, not finding a solution, or getting engulfed in the emotion rather than using the emotion as a signal. All this takes place consciously or unconsciously.

In addition, self-doubt weakens our resistance and our mental immunity. It makes us more susceptible to the mind diseases that are out there. As soon as we become vulnerable, irrational emotions, like fear and anxiety and irrational thoughts, step in like a virus. When untreated, they start spreading all over our whole self.

To check for self-doubt, we can check for the viral infection we are suffering. Are we functioning based on a pattern of unhealthy thinking that is not based on facts? Are we functioning based on a series of unreasonable emotions? For example, we can question our self to see how many times we have started a relationship, either romantic or friendship, out of the fear of being lonely, fear of not fitting in, and/or fear of rejection. We can evaluate, to see what came out of such a relationship. We will start to notice a pattern. The relationships that start because of a type of fear are usually not meaningful, and are either temporary or purely empty. That's why we keep jumping from one to another. We are searching for that fulfillment, but if we don't know how to find it, we will end up exactly where we started. That is why we need to take a moment and start from within. Do we even know what we're looking for? Is it based on something we saw in a movie or the cover of some magazine, or is it really what our inner core is asking for? What steps are we talking to get what we want? Are our expectations reasonable, and what are they based on? So, as you can see, all the questions have a base-oriented approach to them, because the surface's time is over. We have come to realize that it is not working, so it's time to go back to the root, learn, and move forward.

A relationship has to start based on a sense of internal connection, and that can only be accomplished after we have worked on our self-doubt and irrational emotions, including fears. Once we do this, we will start learning that there is no such thing as being lonely, because, in a way, we are what we searching for in others, and everything we are searching for, and trying to get, from the external world so that we won't feel lonely, it is already within us. If we get there and work on releasing our fear, any relationship we will have with others is not based on neediness, but on a sense of true love. Such a relationship can create a nurturing and learning atmosphere for everyone involved. It turns into a flawless micro-system of its own. After all, anything based on positive intentions creates positive, anything based on negative intentions creates negative.

When it comes to our ways of thinking and whether they are rational or irrational, we need to evaluate where they are coming from. Was it a misconception we picked up during our upbringing, which was never challenged and just stayed with us? If so, how is it affecting us? Is it limiting, or does it help us with our growth process? One of the most common global ways of irrational thinking is the black-and-white thought process.

When I have a presentation, I'm sometimes asked questions in the "Is it this or is it that?" category. I have had questions like, "Is it evolution or creation?" Or, "Is the point of life to be happy or to learn?"

My answer is usually the same, "These are connected, not separate. They are continuous, and on the same spectrum."

Again, as evolved minds, we need to start thinking how things are linked. We need to pay attention to how they cooperate with each other. To those types of questions, my more specific response would be something like, "So how about evolution was created, and creation is a part of evolution?" Or "To be happy one must learn, and to learn one must be happy." Or how about this: "Evolution was created by evolution."

What if we start thinking that way, giving them an infinite taste of reality, putting them together rather than seeing them as separates? Wouldn't that be more interesting, and wouldn't that, considering the knowledge and factual information that we have today, make more sense?

In today's world, with the technology we have, it's as easy to be informed as it is to be manipulated. It's really a matter of personal choice which route we want to take. With one click, we can receive a wealth of information, with that same click we can get engulfed into all sort of mind diseases. It takes pushing the right bottom on the remote, picking that right title, and talking to that right person to be informed and to learn. Information all the way from billions of years ago to what future may bring is as accessible as anything else.

Science is becoming more lucid to the general mind, where before it was a separate entity, only open to a limited number of people. In addition, science is explaining more and more of what was once identified as "God," this unlimited source of essence. I see scientists exploring deeper into how the human brain functions, why it categorizes things, how it is evolving, and how it relates to others. There are always new discoveries turning previous mysteries into facts. Physics and quantum physics have taken us way beyond our wildest imagination as to the sources of the unseen. Astronomy is giving us a bigger picture of this magnificent universe. Psychology is opening the door to our true identity and soul with self-discovery. And the more we learn, the more we wonder about the beauty of this existence. Whether we call it God or something else, one thing clear is that today's God is not the limited, weak, retrieving God that our incomplete mind was trying to identify with. Besides, the more evolved our mind gets, the more whole and multifaceted this God gets. As we move forward, we notice that all the things we categorized as bad vs. good are simply the mechanisms of a perfect self-efficient and designed structure that is moving forward. And that bad and good are individual perceptions of how imbalances function. For each person, what separates her from her core is a bad thing and what gets her closer to her core is a good thing. So, it is different for each individual, depending on multidimensional factors.

At the end, the more we can see how the world functions, the more we learn that it is a combination of all the opposites we once tried so hard to separate, and they are, after all, completing each other. They always have and always will, but we are starting to understand it just now. Who knows what we'll understand 100 years from now? Compare now with 100 years ago.

So, keep your mind open and allow yourself to feel amazed, since there is still more to come. And, for those of us who want to know if we can scientifically become spiritual, we always have been, but were not able to understand it. But, as our frontal lobe is becoming more functional, and we become more rational and logical, we want to understand what we feel. When feelings related to the concept of who I am get started, we want to understand what it is and where it is coming from. We don't just want to take in information that is out of date or does not make sense. It has to make sense. We want more than that. So we look to science to give us more answers. As we demand more, science gives more. As science provides more, we get even thirstier, and the cycle feeds itself. We become more in tune with facts and evidence to show us where we live, where we came from, and whether we are heading somewhere.

To finalize this chapter, we come to realize that science and spirituality are really parts of the same spectrum, not separate, but complimenting each other. One without the other may become nothing more than another source of distraction. They have to learn ways to work together, and we have to learn ways to make them work together.

Beauty of Existence

I was whispering with existence
It was nearby but I felt a distance

It was looking at me with compassion
I felt an exquisite sense of passion

I told her of life, of its ups and its downs
I showed her my heart, its bottom and its crown

Like a compassionate mother, with an unconditional love
She listened to my secrets, from beyond and above

She was quiet, but I could hear
There was fog around, but she was clear

After I was willing to open the door of reflection
I sensed an intense feeling of connection

After I understood this connection
I sensed a joy of having a direction

A peaceful presence overcame me
A peacefulness that felt infinite

I came to realize that serenity was within
All I had to do was dig in

Poem by Roya R. Rad

Conscious vs. Unconscious

Many of us have heard the words conscious and unconscious, but few of us have tried to understand their meaning. The trick here is that we can't be aware of what is deep down within our unconscious unless we start understanding and excavating into it, deeper and deeper. Then we will notice that we are entering a seemingly endless tunnel, and every time we think we've finished the process, there comes another door wide open. Many of us spend a lot of time trying to avoid this excavation, as if there is something better out there to chase. We make up a fantasy life and try to escape the truth. We repress and avoid anything that may be painful to face, not knowing that because we avoid it does not mean it does not exist, and sometimes feeling pain is the most awakening experience. What we avoid and repress exists within us and is in full control of us; they are keeping us slaves.

Going back to the subject of conscious and unconscious, I've touched on this subject before, but will elaborate. There are three main elements: the ego, unconscious at a more personal level, and an unconscious at a more collective level. The ego is a sense of consciousness that emerges early in life, maybe even before birth. The threat that the ego's emergence may bring is one-sidedness and bias; the inability to see both sides. We can think of an ego as the doorkeeper who decides what perceptions, thoughts, and feelings come into consciousness. Ego's attempt is to sustain a sense of consistency within our personality to give the individual a sense of identity, connection, and stability. The personal unconscious is a storage area for life's experiences, including repressed and forgotten experiences. Nothing fades away here. A complex is an unconscious element formed when the individual gets preoccupied with something which affects all her thought and behavior. The part beyond our personal unconscious, which is more of a united unconscious, is rooted in our evolutionary past, which offers an outline of our body and personality. This part of the unconscious seems to rise above time. It is the mind's idea, and neglecting it may come out as phobias, delusions, and other psychological disorders.

Carl Jung said that the personal unconscious and repressed material that what we deny the existence of will control us, and what we acknowledge we can control. When we become aware of our repressed and unconscious material, we become aware. Therefore, it is not unconscious anymore. We have recognized a part of us. We may not like it, but realization leads to acceptance, and only after acceptance comes the decision to change. Once we understand a part of us that we don't like or that gives us pain, we can choose to change or release it. It is, in a way, as simple as that. We are not its slaves anymore.

Self-reflection is the key to understanding. We may ask ourselves questions like, Why do we choose friends or associates whom we think are taking advantage of us? Why do we keep on wanting to be close to or get approval of someone who keeps hurting us? Why do we keep getting angry with someone we love? Why do we act impulsively, and then regret it? Why do we procrastinate? On the surface, it seems like we are running our life through conscious thought and words, but there is a gap; the gap between the conscious and beyond. Whatever feelings, thoughts, and expressions we are scared to talk about openly or to face and admit to, goes to the unconscious and is buried there, not knowing that they will spill out, one way or another. Words that slipped off the tongue, procrastination, addictive and self-destructive behaviors, too much neediness, repetitive acts that are damaging, hostile comments or feelings toward others, aggressive acts, and health problems are just some of the side effects of the unconscious that is not attended.

If, however, we become more curious and try to understand this unconscious, we can improve the quality of the life we live. We can connect with the more transparent side. The opportunity is there. What separates us from it is us and nothing else. We can go as far as we choose to go. Even better, we can make it our life's goal to get there. Working through the unconscious has to be done indirectly through dreams, behavioral signals, and associations. If we try to approach the unconscious directly, our fear and denial will step in and try to block us. We have to find a middle ground to enter into it.

Some beginning psychotherapists and the general public think that if we tell people what is wrong, we can fix it, and that since we are supposed to be rational creatures we should be able to fix it. The problem with this is that if there is no root-oriented approach. Even if the behavior is changed, the root may resurface another way. So, we have to go back to the source.

To use an example of how the unconscious may affect us, if we have a lot of unresolved anger toward someone and we deny that we have any negative feelings toward her or, even worse, we pretend that we love such a person with all we have, then the anger starts getting repressed and has no way of coming out and expressing itself the right way. But it is very much there, and getting denser and denser as it is being ignored. It keeps pushing us here and there without us knowing what hit us. It may come out as other negative feelings, like jealousy, inner sadness, hidden resentments, self-doubt, or the like. Or we may get angry for reasons that are irrational, so we are targeting it at the wrong source. In such a case, this anger is controlling an aspect of our life without us even noticing.

Entering and discovering the unconscious side can help us in overcoming what we don't know about ourselves. As we do this more, we become more aware of our motives, we get less consumed with denial, and we get closer to our authentic self. The closer we get to our authentic self, the less pressured and more liberated we feel.

We term them separate, but in reality conscious and unconscious are not separate from each other. Unconscious is the more transparent side of the conscious; it is simply a reflection. As we move further into it, we keep reaching more and more transparency, and we discover a side of us we didn't know existed. But, in a way, we may notice that we have reached the truly worthy side and we can't help asking ourselves, why did we keep running away from this? What else did I have to do that was so important? And then we may even feel a little silly. But it's okay. Once we get there, we can move on and let the journey began.

Disparity

Me and you are from separate entities
Don't come in mine, don't enmesh our identities

Yours is small
Full of ego and that is all

Mine is immense
There is no fence

It is free
I just want to be

I plan to fly
I don't want to live a lie

I aim to go high like an Eagle
I don't intend to live like a Beagle

Flies are everywhere
It is those soaring high that are rare

Your fear will keep you a slave
My essence tells me to be brave

Your beliefs become your chain
My beliefs are not my source of restrain

Poem by Roya R. Rad

Priceless Things Are Sometimes Concealed. Are We Searching Hard Enough?

Sometimes, with advertisements, marketing strategies, technology, and image-making trainings, it may seem hard to realize what is real and what is not. At points, it may appear like the ones who try the hardest to represent a certain image are the ones farthest from their own truth. So, how do we know that what we see is what we get? How do we learn to distinguish the dust from the diamond? After all, there is so much dust that it can make our vision blurred.

Diamonds are hidden many miles below the ground, and we have to dig to get to them. Diamonds don't sell cheap. All of us see many examples on a daily basis, indicating that what is the most popular is not necessarily the best; it could be quite the opposite. People would do anything to get others to pay attention, mostly for personal gains like power, money, or fulfilling some sort of a basic need, sometimes at a heavy cost to others.

At the end, it all goes back to the same concept of self-reflection. The question we have to ask ourselves is, what it is that we are searching for? And then put in the time and effort to find it. We can't just accept it because we are imitating others, we can't just follow because something is popular, we can't just accept what is presented without knowing the intent of the presenter, we have to discover the truth and follow its lead. This needs work. If we are not willing to do the work, we can't expect any more than we receive.

Throughout this book, I've discussed quality vs. quantity a few times. I've also said that quantity is usually a thing of the ego, while quality is more a thing of the higher self. Now, it seems like those who want to catch our attention do it in a way to make us think that because they have more, they are better. The question then is, more of what? More of ignorance does not make one better. More of the shallow does not make it deep. Thousands of sheep are still sheep, nothing more. Just because there are more sheep does not make them into lions. We need to ask ourselves what it is that we are demanding, because in any society it is usually what is demanded that creates what is presented. We see online sites and how they emphasize so much how many clicks or followers they have; we are not sure why it is that it matters, since it does not mean much, but some may still think more means better. This could go all the way from small things to the bigger ones. How many times have we heard of a presenter with thousands, hundreds of thousands, or even millions of listeners who turned out to be non-genuine, bringing out misguidance, confusion, and disappointment to their members? How many times have we seen opinionated people who have a personal and one-sided agenda attracting a large number of people?

Now, there is no question that there are always those who have both a good quality and good quantity, and sometimes that may very well go together. There are many things that fall into that category and are well deserving of what they get. But my point here is to help bring awareness of the fact that just one or the other does not mean anything. We still have to look deep to see whether what we see is what we get. Just because a large group wants it does not mean a thing, if that group has similar minds and keep on following each other.

Overall, just like it is harder to find a pure diamond than a tainted one, it also could be harder to find authenticity, because in a way it seems like we are encouraging fakeness. Pure diamonds are rare and usually hidden from the average. For those of us serious seekers, however, it is accessible. We just need to pay attention.

I had a friend working in the marketing industry telling me the secrets marketers may use to make a good show. Now, I have no concern if it is a show to be put on, and it is what it says it is to be. But what about those who claim they have something that they don't? What about those who seem to spend more time and money making a show that claims to have something deeper to offer? What about those who manipulate our senses and our perceptions to misguide us? The answer would be that they may very well do that, and we do not have much control of how we change the way they approach the situation. However, we do have control over how we want to react to it. We can always get well-informed, move above the sense stimulation, and see what really is and what is not. It is a personal choice.

This friend also shared with me how some of the public presenters have pre-recorded voice with pre-written statements and that all they have to do is to go over to the microphone and imitate the images they see or hear through a mini microphone and a screen. Now, I wasn't that surprised to hear that. But what I am concerned with is that if we create an image that is a phony us, and hope that people will come to idealize us into something superhuman, how do we expect people to measure up to that image? Wouldn't it just create more anxiety and insecurity if it is not done truthfully? And wouldn't it just create a general sense of disappointment and mistrust in the real thing when more and more of the tricks are revealed? And by creating a phony image, aren't we making it harder for people to see that we are all human, we all have struggles that we need to deal with on a daily basis, and that it is our sincerity with ourselves and the world around us that makes us truly valuable?

The good news is that people are getting more and more informed about this, they are getting smarter and questioning things more. They are learning to look at the unseen, and at motivations behind behaviors. They seem to care less about the expensive image and look more into what is going on behind the scenes. They seem to focus less on the cover and more on the content. With that awareness comes a shift of change, and we get what we demand. They are showing more interest in the root rather than the shallow. That is the work of a higher self and not an ego. Remember, ego wants it easy, so it looks for an easy explanation. Higher self is well aware that to have anything of value, one must work toward having it, and that nothing truly valuable comes too easily. The higher self takes the image into consideration, but looks into the unseen for consistency and truthfulness.

But we still have a lot of work to do. Today, there seems to be so much competition over whose image is a more certain way that there may be no place left for the simple. Considering that the best is sometimes found in the simplest, how are we to know? How are we to find the authentic sources, how are we to know which information is right and which one is not, and how are we to know if the expensive advertisement is consistence with the force behind it?

Anyone can make a fancy website, hire a connected publicist, do the expensive advertisement, but really how do we know we're getting the real thing? How do we know that what a so-called guru is claiming to have found is coming from the right source? Do we go with how large an audience they have? That could be very misleading, since many of the fake ones have a large number of followers or participants, since they learn more skills to manipulate. What then? Well, the answer is that there is no easy way out, but there is a way. As I've said, over and over again, as easy it is to get manipulated; it is also easy to get informed. So, educating ourselves is the key. Learning, learning, and more learning. Also, we should never be scared to ask why before entering any sort of activity. That is the only way we can escape being infected by this viral cycle of manipulation and stop being a follower. We need to demand to know.

At the end, we have to start learning to pay attention, but go beyond what our five senses tell us. If we limit ourselves to just the five senses, we may miss out on a lot. There is so much to discover in the unseen, the unconscious, and beyond. Again, remember that diamonds are found 100 miles below the surface of the Earth, but dirt and dust are everywhere and easy to see and touch. So, if we want diamonds, not dirt, we have to start excavating.

Inner Freedom

Freedom is a special inner concession
We can have access by self confession

When the door of wakefulness unlocks
When we get rid of any sort of blocks

Something pours, some form of a drift
As if we let go of a long time heavy lift

We feel lighter and lighter
The outlook looks brighter

Our vision becomes more clear
As we learn to release our fear

Fear of rejection, fear of isolation
Turn into a complete sense of admiration

We get to a center place in creation
Where there is no sense of frustration

It is were we belong, there is no temptation
All that is, is a feeling of dedication

It is where we glance from the above
That we know what it means to feel love

The love was with us all along
We were just distracted for too long

Poem by Roya R. Rad

Let's All Dance, Shall We?

Once the process of self-excavation starts, surprising changes come along. These changes have to be celebrated so that we can achieve a level of self-liberation. Self-liberation is not being boundless, but is a sense of inner freedom. Freedom from unbearable pain that we create for ourselves, freedom from irrational thoughts and behaviors that enslave us, freedom from irrational feelings, like guilt, that make us do things we don't want to do or stop doing things we want to do, freedom from unreasonable fear, and freedom from neediness. It takes self-discipline to achieve this self-liberation.

So, dance and enjoy the process!

When we free ourselves from the baggage, we are free to go with the flow, because we find our role in this life. We become one with what we are, and we take the path it designs for us. Until then, there is work to be done.

While changes are happening they may be uncomfortable to us or people around us, so we need to give ourselves a reasonable adjustment time. In a way, the change may push us toward moving out of a certain comfort zone. If other people have been in that comfort zone with us, and they are not open to changing and moving forward, they may feel threatened by our move.

Such people may want to push us to stay with them. They may reject us, and they may impose guilt and fear upon us, but if we are aware of what we are doing, none of that will come between us and where we are set to go. Courage is a built-in tool within the system. As change occurs, we may move from one zone to another, but this change is not circular. It is an expanding kind of a change. As we move, we may face many challenges, but at the same time we learn new skills to deal with them. That, by itself, strengthens our mind's muscle. The more we practice, the stronger it gets. How far we want to go is up to us and our internal sense of motivation, but the one thing we have to find is a way to dance on the way there; dance to the music of existence. We have to enjoy our moments, feel the feelings, including the joy, and feel what it is to be content, do our best at any given moment, accept the consequences, learn, and move forward. We also have to learn how to find harmony between our dance moves and existence's music. We have to connect the two.

We should remember that it is not perfection that we are chasing. Every time we get into this illusive cycle of chasing perfection, we may be limiting ourselves. Perfection can sound like something with an end. There is no end to chasing our wholeness. It is an unlimited process, since once we enter a zone and discover it, another zone opens up. Again, remember the onion; peel one layer, and there comes another. If you think this is too much work, think again. What else do you really have to do? When you have answered that question, think about it.

As we move farther, we see ourselves moving faster and our baggage starts to get lighter, since self-doubt, anxiety, fear, irrational thoughts, and out of balance feelings seem to vanish, little by little. We learn how to let go of unnecessary distractions and focus more. We learn to be more honest to ourselves, we pay attention to quality, not quantity, we value what is really important and let go of the extras, and we find ourselves in a state of being awake and aware.

We start to live through our essence, not for providing an

image to others. That is when our uniqueness starts to surface, and that is when we discover the creativity within, or a love for it. We become aware of our core, and this awareness expands as we move forward. In the meantime, we feel intense emotions and feel them fully; we attend to our feelings, but don't let them engulf us. Instead, we read into what they are communicating to us, we feel the feeling, get the message, and deal with it reasonably. We don't carry on anything that is not productive, including intense emotions, feelings, or thoughts for too long. We do not let them consume us. We seem to find the ability to be able to find gratitude for simple things, we seem to be able to cherish the real beauty, and we seem to find more compassion for the totality of life. If all of us get there, there is no need for any of us spending so much time cleaning up other people's messes, since the side-effects of people detaching from their essence will be affecting all of us, one way or the other. Each one of us will play the role she has without trying to be someone else, and when one gets there, she usually gives more than she receives. That would be a world of harmony. Let's all aim for the time in which everything we do is nothing more than a collective living.

To become whole, a drop of water in the ocean with the same qualities as the ocean, and to be able to get to a place of dancing in the water while going through the journey of life, we have to learn self-control, and we have to discover a passion for learning and being curious. Self-control helps us focus more on the right path that belongs to us without too much interruption. Learning helps us not be fooled by imitators, not limit ourselves with invalid knowledge, not to be a follower, and to trust our own understanding rather than letting others tell us what is best for us. We want to get to a place where we are not slaves anymore. We are the master of our own existence. At that point, our gift of free will is working for us to get to our ultimate reality. We are working from our whole self. There is no restraint or limitation in the whole; it is whole, a combination of everything, and we are in charge of it and where we want to take it.

As I said in the previous chapters, with today's progress in science, and with the new discoveries in many areas, like biology, neuroscience, psychology, chemistry, physics, including quantum physics, etc., we are getting much closer to understanding what we are made of, who we are, and where we may be heading. Spirituality seems to be finally making sense, even for intellectuals. The unseen is looking for a more transparent reflection of what we do see. For example, psyche, in many ways, has similar actions and reactions that the body has, but we can't see it because there are invisible forces working to shape it.

We are noticing more and more that having a closed mind and living from a limited sense of being are going to make us into uninformed and selfish elements of life, who miss out on a lot rather than being full participants. If we could only stop separating things from one another and could see that they all are on a continuum and complement each other, how much easier would life be? How much time we would save by only doing that?

To go back to the human concept, as I mentioned before, the psyche is just a more transparent form of the body, and it has similar ingredients. It has similar defense mechanisms, cancerous cells, viral infections, need for equilibrium and inner harmony, and need for healthy mental nutrients to function best. As we learn more about how the invisible elements work to affect the visible ones, we learn more about how action/reaction works. Sometimes, it may seem like everyone is talking about this action/reaction, but at the same time we keep seeing more people with negative impacts on their lives and, as a result, on others and the world. We see unproductively, aggression, crimes, prejudice, greediness, racism, violence in all shapes and forms, and we wonder whether we are walking the walk and following the talk. We see people going so far to show something they are truly not. Or we see others whose pleasing side of them gets the best of them and leaves them no energy to find their authenticity. The world seems to be full of mind viruses, and since viruses copy themselves and are contagious, we seem more than ever to need mental immunity and strength. In each corner of our mind, we are continuously being exposed to others viruses, how we should live, how we should dress, how we should spend our money, how we should vote, how we should choose our destiny. If our defense system is not strong enough to realize which ones to invite in and which ones to push back, we are in for a long and bumpy ride. We have to spend so much time undoing the damage that there is hardly any time left to build.

Just as the body's immune system has the ability to evaluate the body and remove attackers both innately and through acquisition, the same is true about our psyche's immune system. If we can get to a place where we have access to our deeper self, we can access more of this innate immune system. However, we have to gain a type of specialized immunity which can recognize and remember foreign agents and assess them for being fit. We need to learn to bring out our more mature defenses to be able to target and get rid of the more advanced attackers. Attackers may be any sort of mind virus or disease that can make us and our mind weak, distract us from our path and lessen our focus, encourage us to believe we need something that we don't, and encourage us to make unwise decisions that may harm us in the short or long term. We want to get to a point of strength where we say. "Please keep you bowl of waste to yourself, and stop infecting me with it. I want to know the truth. I want to see what is going on. I want to look at the bigger picture of life. I want to function from my higher self rather than from my needy and immature one. I want to rise above events and look at the root. I want to have an opinion, but based on facts and knowledge, and with all I want, I can't afford to carry your waste with me."

When it comes to having opinions, too many of us have opinions that we have no clue where they came from. They are not factually based, and it almost seems like we repeat a number of words to show an image of intelligence. Who knows, maybe those words are rooted in our mind's virus rather than an informed state of being. Sometimes the less we know of something, the more opinionated we seem to become about it. It seems like our ego is using yet another tool to want to prove we know more, or we are right and others are wrong, or that we are smarter, or that this is the only way we can feel like we belong to a group, namely people who have the same opinion.

It is important to check and re-check continuously to see whether it is the ego that is at work, or the higher self. The higher self has ideas which are based on knowledge and facts and a bigger picture of existence, rather than a selfish state. She only wants to share them to enjoy sharing and to connect and to potentially benefit others who can receive. Ego's intent is to prove to others something of a superior image, something like, "Hey look at me, I'm better," without having a basis for the claim. Again, the key here is to bring out the higher self to be in charge of the ego and to learn to turn opinions from being limited and baseless to being boundless and factual. Having the privilege of free speech in a system does not mean we open our mouth and let anything come out of it. This privilege must be gained through knowledge and understanding. The more we learn to do that, the less we sense a need to prove to others that they are wrong and we are right. If we feel there is no connection, we let go and move on.

To go back to the concept of dancing, to dance, we must learn the dance movements, how the moves work, find a natural rhythm within our body, and find synchronization between our body parts. A good dancer pays no attention to the audience and the outside world, but focuses on her inner pace. After learning, practicing, and focusing, a good dancer will have the ability to flow with the music with a sense natural rhythm, while enjoying every move.

If we want to be good dancers of life, we must learn to take the steps right and do them from a center point within; a center point that is hidden but yet available. We must find a balance point within, a sense of wholeness, and a joy for love and learning; a balance point between rationality and intuition, external and internal clues, knowledge and heart, mind and soul, conscious and unconscious, and all opposites within. We must celebrate our wholeness and stop picking and choosing what is easy to grasp. We must learn to find joy in loving and learn how to love, since love is the purest form of emotion. While we are doing this, we must be exclusive with the song we want to dance with. Too many choices can only generate turmoil and disturb the rhythm in which we want to dance. We have to make a choice and learn to dance with it. Once we reach that, and once we feel self-liberated, there is only dancing to do.

At the end, it is worth repeating that in order to be a high quality dancer, we have to be healthy in many ways, be guiding our body parts to work together in synchronization, let no distractions in, focus on the move, and go with the rhythm of the music. We have to learn to be dancing with the flow of life.

So, let's all dance, shall we?

Self Value

You turn into what you hear
So sort out what goes in your ear

You turn out to be what your eyes observe
So ensure what you see is what they deserve

You grow to be what you've believed
So make certain you are not being deceived

Your free choice can take you to infinity
Do you choose the edge or the divinity?

You become with whom you interact
So make sure you know whom to attract

When you get rid of useless distraction
You gain a sense of inner satisfaction

You appreciate what is vital
You let go of the shallow title

Poem by Roya R. Rad

Brain, Evolution, and Free Will

Scientists have reported that if human species survives, the brain will continue to evolve, due to the pressure of natural selection. Researchers who analyzed sequence variations in two genes that regulate brain size in humans gathered data indicating that main variations in the genes occurred at around the same time as the origin of culture, language, and agriculture. This change gave advantages.

Based on the research on 90 individuals, and then the same done on 1,000 from different ethnic backgrounds, researchers found that what they call halogroups occur at a frequency far higher than that expected by chance. Halogroups are broken down haplotypes, and haplotypes are blocks of linked sequences of differences between different individuals. It is a distinct genetic variant of the gene.

They further report that natural selection has speeded up the haplogroup they label as haplogroup D. Haplogroup D occurred more in Europeans and related populations like Iberians, Basques, Russians, North Africans, Middle Easterners, and South Asians. This, however, was found at a lower rate in East Asians, sub-Saharan Africans, and New World Indians. Haplogroup D appeared well after the emergence of modern humans about 200,000 years ago. The timing seems to coincide with modern humans, agriculture, settled cities, and written language. These researchers hypothesize that the geographic basis and circumstances surrounding the spread of the haplogroups may have occurred in Europe or the Middle East, and was extended by migrations.

Researchers have found two genes that indicate evidence of selection in the evolutionary history of the human species and that also show evidence of ongoing selection in humans. It is important to emphasize that these findings should not be used to assume one ethnic group is more evolved than another, but it can be taken as an average impact of such variants. It is giving us an understanding of the origin. For example, just because there is one gene that makes us a little taller doesn't mean that we all will be taller. There are other environmental and multidimensional factors that affect this process. This, however, emphasizes that the human evolutionary process may continue to move forward under the pressure of natural selection. This report was cited by the Howard Hughes Medical Institute.

To discuss our brain, when looking at how much of our brain potential we are using, studies indicate that human brain is a whole system consisting of about 33 microbrains. It is a highly organized system. Each of these microbrains is responsible for its own functioning, capacity, and memory. For example, there is one microbrain responsible for vision, hearing, balance, smell, taste, mathematics, language, imagination, logic, music or art, etc. Some of these microbrains are located in the right hemisphere, while others are in the left, but each has extended branches to the other hemisphere, so they are connected. But the main function of the whole brain is to bring orderliness, organization, and assimilation between these microbrains.

Now to think about how much of our brain's capacity we are using, when people categorized as geniuses are researched, it has been shown that most are using only one of these microbrains completely, making it about 4% of their whole brain. For example,

Einstein used the full capacity in math, Angelo in imagination (artistic), Russo in argument (philosophical), Mozart in music, etc. These people were able to use about 100% of one microbrain. It is also worth noting that most of these individuals may have suffered from some form of brain disorder or brain unrest. For example, Mozart had epilepsy and Angelo had schizophrenia. Reading about this type of information makes us wonder how far can we really go, if we want to reach our full potential and find a balance between these microbrains.

Then comes the discussion of afterlife and brain activities. The subject of afterlife has been neglected by science until recently. In a more recent study, doctors from George Washington University Medical Faculty recorded brain activities of patients who were dying from critical illnesses like cancer or heart attack. These doctors reported that moments before the patients died, they experienced a burst in brain wave activity, according to their EECs.

The subject of death has been avoided by the science community in the past, and left to religion to explain, mostly unsuccessfully, but that seems to be changing with a shift in demand and awareness. Both science and religion are recognizing a need to unite and evolve to help individuals comprehend the process, which is undeniably a part of everyone's life. If one goes against the other rather than working together, they may create more uncertainty and misunderstanding in the long run.

At the end, it seems like there are many parts of our brains we are not using, so through evolution, are we going to use more even at a faster speed? The evidence indicates that we are using our brain more than before, so we can't help thinking that it will probably continue on the same path. Especially now that we are learning more about the brain's capacity, the more we learn, the more we want to expand. And then one wonders, where would that take us? The answer seems to be that if used with integrity, it will take us to wondrous places; if not, wonder can change to tedious. It is a matter of our choice and where we want to take our free will.

Free will seems like a treasure that we are given access to, depending on our level of growth. If we pay attention, we can get to a point of inner liberation, where at the same time we will be more in control of how we feel, think, act, and lead our life. We are able to access this free will more. The more free will we have, the more we have the ability to experience life to the fullest and according to one's self-growth requirements. When we get to that point, we seem to have greater inner balance and harmony. We value what we hold, and make sure it is used to the fullest, and in the best possible way. This includes our brain's components, our personality's elements and all else we possess, from internal to external. To be able to hold something as being valuable, we have to learn about it and understand it first.

At the end, free will is not a free gift that is granted just because we categorize ourselves as human. We may think that we posses it, while we are nothing more than slaves to our own limiting actions and thoughts. Free will can be achieved, like anything else, by accomplishing certain aspirations. The more we achieve these aspirations, the more free will we can sense and have. Our evolved brain can be used as a tool in helping us experience more and more of our free will. A person who functions from a more evolved state of being makes sure that what she holds is nurtured and grows. Any blockage in the process creates inner conflict which will be expressed externally.

Restraining the self

When you shut yourself to reality
You restraint your sense of morality

You shake off your state of duality
You live in part instead of in totality

You elude the feelings of vitality
Truthfulness fades away from your mentality

You are alien to the need for spirituality
You are a stranger to the idea of commonality

This cycle of detrimental abnormality
Becomes your way of life, your modality

Time has come to release the irrationality
Only then you can see and walk toward liberality

Poem by Roya R. Rad

Wholeness and an Evolved Human Being

I should clarify that by the word evolution, I do not necessarily mean we are descended from monkeys. That is not the point of this book, and is less relevant than we may think to the general concept of evolution. However, by evolution I do mean what both science and common sense are solidly indicating, that we are advancing as a whole human being. For some of us, it seems faster than others, but it is happening.

As we move forward in this process of life, we seem to be able to understand what it means to have a "self," and what we can do to start learning more and more about it. While growing, the more mature we become, and the more we find the ability to be objective when observing a situation. Most of us are subjective in our judgments, depending on how we were conditioned. We judge things according to our modified, biased, and limited individual mind that has been molded according to our family, our culture, our religion, our government, our surroundings, etc. A more mature mind learns about all of these, does not deny or avoid any of them, since they are a part of her, and understands them. Only after that we can make the choice of rising above and beyond these aspects and see things from a more expanded view. When we reach that stage, the means we were brought up with are not limiting obstacles anymore, but may even become useful. When there, we can see through things from a broader perspective, making it more objective, and we may be capable of making more rational decisions based on facts, not perceptions.

Many of us may think or hope we are free of conditioning, when in reality we are not, whether consciously or unconsciously. We are conditioned one way or the other, and it can constrain our horizon in many ways if we don't get to the level of awareness we need to realize that. To be objective, not to be selfish when viewing the world, not to be influenced by personal feelings, personal interpretations, or prejudices, and to be going forward based on facts, information, and detail takes a lot of sweat, and many of us are just not interested in putting in that much effort. We are too opinionated about things we only know on the surface, and spend a lifetime defending them, not for the purpose of sharing, but for satisfying the ego.

As we evolve, we may learn that there is a unity when we get past the conditioning. We may learn that we don't need to do things for the fear of hell or reward of heaven. We understand that heaven and hell are nothing more than an inner experience that reflects who we are and how we view and experience our life, and that we carry these perceptions with us. We may sense that hell would be a self-imposed agony and heaven would be a self-created ecstasy. Whatever the wise men have been trying to communicate to us for centuries is being discovered by science, and we are able to comprehend it now more than ever. We can analyze and make sense of it. It sure feels good. We find ourselves being satisfied by the thirst we have had for so long to learn about who we are, where we come from, and where we might be heading. And we find more need to be curious. Now the question on some people's mind is whether curiosity killed the cat. The answer would be maybe, but she sure had a life more worth living than an indolent cat that just sat there and expected to be served.

If we get jammed and stop growing, we will fall behind. The more we fall behind, the more we feel distanced and lose motivation. We may even go to a state of nothingness with no effect, no positive impact, and at times leaving our mark with negative ones. None of us really wants to choose to go to a state of nothingness. We go there because we lack the necessary endeavor. All humans are innately built for growth. We want to move forward, but ignoring and neglecting the higher self and avoiding the depth can cause this built-in feature to become dysfunctional. Ignorance is a dangerous disease, and can blind us from the truth.

I've said this before, but it is worth repeating that a part of being human is to experience feelings and emotions and find a way to balance them. It is not about being happy all the time. That could turn into being manic or, even worse, escaping any kind of pain at all costs. It is also not about being sad all the time. That would turn into depression and could be debilitating. It is about experiencing feelings, letting emotions set in, learning what they are trying to communicate, and finding a channel to deal with them rather than being swallowed by them. It is about being in control and how one learns to deal with these feelings and emotions, and how one can read their signals and act on them.

As an evolved mind, we can't help but be more in tune with our feelings and emotions and, at the same time, be affected by the pain and joy of others. Simultaneously, we learn ways not to carry these feelings or emotions for too long. For example, when we see a child suffering, we may cry as if we just saw our own child suffer, we may even lose a little of sleep over it, but instead of carrying this sadness and turning it into another baggage with no use, we may start asking ourselves, is there anything, no matter how small, that I can do to make an improvement to this situation, directly or indirectly? So we either act positively on the emotion, or release it with a little more awareness of our surroundings. That is why we feel and have emotions. It is a tool for connecting that we can't do without. It is evolving as we evolve. We have labels for more emotions and feelings than we did before. Why some of us keep being engulfed by the tool and forget about why we have it is a good question to ask ourselves.

When discussing wholeness, we notice that it is open to interpretation. To be able to learn what it is to be whole, we need to look into what is personality. Personality has a phylogenetic origin, evolving from a genetically related group of organisms. In addition, personality is an inheritance of memory traces of the past experience of the human race and current environmental conditions. Therefore, the base of personality is something of an ancient, primitive, and collective nature. Personality can be shaped and changed according to other multidimensional and environmental factors. All of these may create a predisposition in individuals to respond to the world in a conditioned way.

Now the question goes back to what is this whole individual? The individual has a personality, the psyche which holds all thought, feeling, and behavior; whether conscious or unconscious. The psyche's responsibility is to be helping us in adapting to and surviving in our environment, in the best possible way. We need to investigate this psyche to open the door to wholeness.

For some, the life's principle could become to develop the concept of this wholeness to its fullest. This is something we are born with and have the potential to reach. It needs a great deal of courage and self-determination, complete confirmation of all that the individual holds, and successful adaptation to universal conditions of existence, to be able to open the door to what this wholeness is capable of offering.

The realization of the innate peculiarity of human beings is a part of the definition of the psych. Overall, as I said previously, our psych has three elements or three levels of consciousness to it, conscious, unconscious, and beyond. Over the course of a lifetime, one should be able to synthesize and maintain equilibrium between these elements within the self. Again, disparity creates conflict, and conflict creates negativity for the self and its surrounding.

Now let's discuss the concept of free will a little more. We may wonder, sometimes, whether free will is a curse or a blessing. The answer is within the concept. Because we have free will, we get to choose whether we want to make it into a good thing or not. Free will gives a certain authority, but a great deal of liability comes along with it. If we use our free will and choose ignorance, we will have negative impact. This negative impact could be conscious or unconscious. The more unconscious, the more intense and hidden the effect.

It may seem confusing when people try to explain humans as a set structure, since in reality there is no magic formula to live from a state of wholeness. The magic is within each individual's hand. There is however, learning and understanding of the mechanisms. We are a combination of many things. We are the most evolved forms of being on earth. That means we have a bit of all that has existed so far. We have the most evolved emotions, feelings, and thoughts. But, most important, we are becoming more aware of our own existence, our role in it, and our surroundings. The more evolved we become, the more expanded this awareness becomes. We have to get ready for it.

Wholeness and living in totality is learning about all our different aspects, accepting them, and then trying to work with them; our shadow or dark side and our light side, our good qualities and bad ones, our weaknesses and strengths, and all that there is to us. Once we accept all these things as they are, we can take control and make any changes we need to. However, if we continue denying and rejecting certain elements within us, because it is too painful to admit to them, creating an elusive pattern and deception, we are giving control to what we are denying.

Wholeness is just that. There is no ending point to wholeness, it is a process filled with awakening and discovering experiences.

Life in general has wholeness to it as well. It is also a combination of everything. We are a reflection of life; the more transparently we live, the purer this reflection and our experience associated with it become. While we pick the path of life that most suits us, we may, at times, take the wrong detours. This is normal, and even needed, sometimes, but as long as we take these detours with awareness and learn something from them, we haven't lost anything. Sometimes, we may find ourselves having to take these detours because that will give us a personal understanding that we would not have received by just being told by others or reading it somewhere. If we open our eyes and mind and learn from every position we are never losing, because the goal is expanding and learning. Therefore, if that is the goal, there are no resentments and regrets; there are only experiences, awareness, and living the process. Regrets come with intentional harms we create for ourselves and others. If we are aware, the chances of us intentionally creating harm lessen.

During the experience of our life, we may realize that many things that happen to us are a result of direct action and reaction. This becomes more apparent as we change our mental defenses from the more primitive ones to more evolved ones. As we cut down on blaming external factors for how we feel inside, we step out of denial and avoidance into awareness and rationality. We can see that there is, after all, a design within this picture-perfect creation we call life. This is not to ignore the fact that there is always a probability factor that may be out of our control and can affect an aspect of our life, but it has much less effect than we give it credit for. If we get to the point of this awareness, we find ways to damage ourselves less and, since we project to others what we have, the less damaged we are, and the less damage we cause. We may even start to notice that many of the obstacles in life that look like huge monsters are nothing more than a shade.

An important element to walking toward a state of wholeness is self-reflection. There are different methods we can go about to self-reflect. We can write down our dreams and try to analyze them. For example, I had a client telling me of a dream he had repeatedly, of a big house that he was decorating to make it look more appealing. He reported decorating it with things like picture frames etc., but it was not getting where he wanted to. When we went deep into the dream, analyzing it from different aspects, and considering the stage at which my client was, it became noticeable that perhaps he needed to renovate the house instead of decorating it, and start working on some of the features that were neglected and fix it starting from the foundation. This he could see as a message from his unconscious. He then connected this with renovation and root-oriented work on his self. He went back to his childhood and started to think about what lead to what, bringing out repressed memories, processing them, feeling the feeling, and letting them release themselves. As he moved into the process, he felt more and more free.

He remembered that he'd stood up strongly for fairness since he was a child, whatever his level of understanding of it was at the time. Since childhood, he had a creative artist within him that was never unleashed. He had a strong sense of compassion for the voiceless. He found some of his weaknesses to be the fact that he was trying hard not to feel a sense of loneliness, as if he had a fear of being lonely. He did not enjoy time with himself, as if he was running away from something within. He always wanted to push himself to be surrounded by many people, even though he also had a need to be by himself sometimes.

After an intense level of self-reflection and celebration of his introvert side, the fear started to vanish. He started to find a balance between his extroversion and introversion. He started to enjoy spending time by himself, as well with others who were rewarding. That is when he discovered more and more of what he was made of, while he continued his social sides and the joy and learning opportunities they presented. It was that inner balance he was looking for. That is when he discovered his artistic side and started to respond. Now, his goal is to get to his full potential while enjoying life. He still has a strong sense of compassion, but tries not to get emotionally entangled in a situation. He has found himself much more able to help a situation when he can control his emotions. That does not mean that he does not feel. He feels intensely, but has found a way to manage the feeling. Anxiety may still kick in, sometimes, especially when the situation is too new or too overwhelming, but that is something he has come to accept, since it is more of a rational and situational anxiety. As a result, he started to feel more comfortable with himself, and later with his relationships, no matter where they took him. Things seemed more natural.

I have explained other methods of self-reflection in previous chapters. It is important for each one of us to examine and see what works and what does not. At the end, it is worth repeating that if we want to get close to understanding our state of wholeness, we need to start walking the walk, following the talk, and learning the process. With determination and effort this task becomes possible.

Possessions

All your possessions do not make you bigger
All you have become is nothing more than a digger

Your belongings are holding you from expansion
All you want is to add another mansion

Living in a palace with an empty mind
Closes you to existence, makes you blind

Closing your eye, you only see the dark
You mistake the grave yard for the park

You forget that you are your own master
You wonder why your heart feels a disaster

You turn into your own design's slave
You start digging your own pointless grave

You desecrate your infinite essence
You ignore the beam and focus on

Poem by Roya R. Rad

How Do We Live From A Wholeness State Of Being?

As days go by and we wonder around our life, we can't help noticing that sometimes we may be chasing what seems like a state of nothingness. We feel empty, we deal with insecurities, and our actions are based on fear and other primitive emotions. We may feel like we were plunged in this life, half full, half empty, not knowing what it is that we are here for and who brought us here. We lack a meaningful motivation. We continuously condition our mind to make sense of what is around us, but may still have a sense of blankness. Some of us may think we want something because others have told us so. At other points, we may feel like we've been spending a lot of time undoing damages rather than building something. Impulse control seems a thing of the mystic world, and happiness is defined as satisfying the continuously deprived drives and urges. We get confused about why we don't feel satisfied and fulfilled. We have so much, but we feel so small. We will do anything externally to feel big, but it just does not seem to work. Then we feel exhausted and overstressed. The cycle continues, and we look for others to come and give us answers to find some sort of healing.

The problem with trying too hard to satisfy the impulses is that the impulse wants something quick. It doesn't have the capacity to think of the long- and short-term consequences of the action. It needs instant gratification, which is supposed to be a thing of the infancy stage, but for the impulse there is no distinction. It is not capable of understanding what it means to delay gratification to weigh out the consequences. That's why we need to step in and control our impulses. The lack of impulse control would take us on detours, consuming too much energy without having the joy of gaining something valuable.

The outside world is a big place. If we cannot concentrate on what we want from it, it can become confusing. We may end up jumping from one thing to the other. We have to single out our life's path and walk that way. If we keep wandering around, we will be wasted. As I said, having too many choices can create perplexity. We need to get to know who we are, pick the road most suited to us, not according to someone else's standards, but for ourselves, focus, take a map, pack up light, and walk the walk. We have to be focused, learn while walking, enjoy what the road offers, and move ahead. The road has enough to offer, if we don't get greedy and take detours to find more, which will only slow us down.

We need to carry a light bag with only what is required. Fear of the future, repressed and unresolved issues of the past, irrational and limiting patterns of thinking, primitive emotions like rage, obsessive and addictive behaviors, anxious and unhealthy relationships will slow us down. We need to work on them and let go of them. The lighter the bag, the faster we can walk. We also need to let go of any unnecessary distractions. In the meantime, we need to use what is offered to discover who we are and how we can advance emotionally, mentally, intellectually and spiritually. That process by itself will create in us a human that is on her way to being content and feeling fulfilled. A content and fulfilled human does not project negativity and is naturally fruitful. The reality of it starts from within. The rest are the mind's conditions.

Tom Campbell, in his book, *My Big Toe*, takes us on a unique journey of existence. The key point of his book, for me, was that we are living this life to learn to live from a low entropy position. This low entropy creates a being who wastes the least amount of energy while being at her most productivity level. This sounds similar to many concepts of psychology. This has to be done through getting to a natural state of being, which comes after all of our extra loads are emptied.

When one really digs into the concept of happiness, one learns that those individuals who have learned to live a life of low entropy are the ones most connected with their life and are the most satisfied. This satisfaction is also representing itself from an external view. From Maslow's perspective, this is the characteristic of self-actualized individuals who seem to have reached a state of low entropy were they take little, give more, are doing what they like, are content with their life, and are productive. And for Carl Jung and his definition of wholeness, it seems to be referring to a low-entropy stage where one learns who she is, and lives from a complete sense of self rather than denying and avoiding the unaccepted parts, which helps her in releasing the unwanted.

Balance is the key to wholeness. One has to be able to find a balance and find a way for her characteristics to work together in harmony; a balance between introvert and extrovert, thinking, feeling, sensation, and intuition. Disparity is the number one source of conflict.

A balance between the extrovert and an introvert is the one in which the psyche's energy is flowing between the person's inner and outer world. Having a touch of introversion is needed for self-reflection and self-discovery, and having a touch of extroversion is needed for interacting with others, connecting, and putting what is learned to practice. Where this balance lies is a unique and personal matter, depending on the person's personality, needs, and potential.

In West, extroversion is considered more as mainstream than introversion. However, in East, it is the other way around. Many creators, writers, poets, and scientists who have added so much to our life were perhaps more often introverts than extroverts. But the downside to not having a balance is that introverts may be more prone to depression, while extroverts may be prone to loss of identity.

In addition to that, we have to look at finding a balance point between our other components, including thinking-feeling-sensation-intuition. Thinking and feeling are the tools that can help us make a decision and judge a situation, more of the rational side, while sensation and intuition are the ones that help us gather information and perceive more of an observational side. When we think, we try to analyze in an objective way to understand the meaning of something. When we feel, we weigh and value a situation subjectively. If we let ourselves feel the feeling, listen to what it has to offer, and then let the thinking side take a role, we may find a more harmonious outcome to the situation. Unfortunately, most people prefer one over the other, creating repression.

When it comes to sensation, it is more of a sensual perception which is practical, realistic, and sensible. While intuition is a hunch, hidden potential, being spontaneous, it is more of a fantasy and imagination of the future. Both perceive, but to have the fuller experience they have to be complementing each other. Again, most people prefer one over the other, generating repression.

We are all trying to find ways to feel fulfilled, joyous, and content, one way or the other. We want to have healthy bonds with people. The definition of a healthy bond vs. an anxious attachment is a subject worth knowing about, which I had discussed in my previous books. You can also find a brief description at the end of this book. Overall, many of us function through fear and guilt or anxious attachments rather than a sense of love.

In some of the third world countries, there seems to be a

lot of focus on spending time together, but not as much on emotional ones. Families may spend a lot of time together doing family activities, but when you ask questions about feelings, deepest fears, and emotional needs, they usually are not very responsive. In the more developed countries, there seems to be more attention and openness toward having an emotional bond, but physical closeness and spending quality time are things that people seem to be struggling with. A happy system is one that has a middle ground of all of the above.

Another important factor that needs to find a balance is the concept of love and discipline. Somewhere in our adult life, we have to become our own parent, bring out our inner child, and give her the love and discipline she may have lacked during her childhood, or to improve upon it. Most people are missing an element of one or the other. Either they did not feel loved, or they lacked some form of discipline. The more love we get, the more we form meaningful connections; the more discipline we get, the more fulfilled our life becomes, since it gives a sense of inner freedom and direction. In this ever-increasingly crowded world, a sense of direction is needed more than ever.

The balance point between love and discipline comes from an authoritative parent. So, we need to bring out that kind of a parent. To explain this more in details, it is worth touching base on what each parenting style is.

There are three main parenting styles, authoritarian, authoritative, permissive.

An authoritarian parent is one who is strict, demanding, gives rules without explanation, punishes for breaking the rule and does not reward for following them, is cold, does not share emotion, and functions based on giving guilt and fear to the child. Such a parent creates the seed of emotional vulnerability, emotional coldness, relationship issues, and low self-esteem in children. Even though many times these children may succeed in life, either through education or in business, because of the high demands parents imposed upon them, and they may grow intellectually, due to the strict and demanding environment with unreasonable expectations, but these individuals are usually emotionally unsatisfied and immature in many ways, with a low sense of self-esteem, self-value and security. Their sense of self-value is very conditional.

On the other side of the parenting spectrum is permissive parenting. This is the very relaxed, and at times careless or lazy, types of parents. There is no real sense of responsibility and obligation that comes with such parenting. These parents are too easy-going, give too much freedom, and have no rules to be followed. Such parents plant the seed of self-esteem, because they give the children a lot of options for exploration, but usually such children, as adults, lack the sense of self-discipline needed to have goals and priorities in life. So they may have good emotional and self-esteem related abilities, but are not as successful as their full potential may have been capable of, due to lack of a sense of direction.

The midpoint of the two is an authoritative parent. Here is where the parent has a balance of reasonable rules suited to the child's age and limitations, and uses nurturing and loving techniques. Rules are explained and understood, there are rewards, both positive and negative, in place for the consequences of behaviors, there is affection, love, a scene of security, and unconditional positive regard and acceptance. These parents are very communicative, they share information, they learn skills, and they encourage full growth. This type of parenting can create a combination of healthy self-esteem and emotional wellbeing, beside encouraging success and intellectual growth.

Now, imagine if you give this sort of attention to your inner child, how much healing can take place?

To end this chapter, the point is to find a center point and work ourselves out from there. We usually do the opposite; we work externally. That's why so much confusion is created for us, by us, within us. It is time to rethink what we have been doing if it does not seem like it has been working.

My God

Don't limit my God
Don't give her a façade

My God is not a God of deprivation
He does not belong to one particular station

My God is a combination
There is no separation

My God is an unrestrained totality
Anything lesser is just my reality

My God gave me an active voice
My God granted me free choice

Poem by Roya R. Rad

Conclusion

There are many questions we have in life, some answered and some not. For example, what does the word tolerance really mean? Do we compromise honesty in the name of tolerance? Does compassion mean we let another's ego step all over us without punishment? Does forgiveness mean we let the perpetrator continue her act? Does being nice mean acting deceitful? Does being strong mean stepping over others? How far is too far, how much is too much, and how little is too little? To answer our many questions, the best way is to open our eyes. When we close our eyes, darkness begins. We need to open our eyes to see the light.

Sometimes it seems like when we open our curtain and look outside the window as it is, we see that we look like the pieces of a chess game. We have different shapes and colors, black, white, soldier, king, queen etc. In a way, it seems like we are all being played by an observer. They are the ones who organize the chess pieces, play with them to see who wins, and compete over it. The chess pieces vary, we see all types. One seems like a homeless guy, one seems like he has two palaces, one is white, one is black, and they are being played by someone else. So, the question we need to ask ourselves is whether we are living like a chess piece, and if so who is playing me? Who is in control of my life and my destiny? Is it me, or someone else? Am I continuously being dragged by outside factors? That's a good question to dig in and work with; a true eye-opening question.

As this poem I wrote related to the subject indicates, we need to find a quiet place within, to find out what goes on outside. Until we do that, we have to find ways to deal with the confusion we are creating for ourselves.

Your silence may deepen you
Watch your silence, it may deepen you
Watch the noise, it may weaken you

You may look at the moon in the water
You may be able to see the slaughter

You may take yourself away from the distance
You may sit down at the window and see the existence

Time is in your hand
Stand up and expand

When you close your eyes, darkness begins
Open your eyes, see the light

Go to the mountain, see the height
Engulf in the light, take a sight

Encounter the reality, feel the delight
Be the reality, stand up upright

I was walking down the street in Shiraz one day and saw a child walking with two men. The child looked about 7 or 8 years old. Something told me to observe the situation. I saw that one of the men, who I thought was the child's father, had a sharp object in his hand, and then I saw him used the object with a force beyond the boy's ability and hit him in the face as hard as he could. I saw the boy bleeding and not even crying. The man walked away with another guy to wherever he was heading as if this was just a part of his daily routine of life. Then I saw the boy's face, such sadness, such a state of helplessness, I don't think he was crying, as if he didn't see a point to crying. I took a deep breath to try to control my emotion, walked toward him, and asked if he was okay.

He had such dark and deep beautiful eyes, he looked at me and shied away. It seemed like he wasn't used to someone caring and coming toward him, so he didn't know how to take it. I tapped his shoulder and asked him if he was okay while I bent my knees to be more his height and not be intimidating. I knew adults might intimidate him, since nobody seemed to be there to defend him, while the one who was supposed to care for him and love him did just the opposite.

I asked him why that man hit him. He said it was his dad, and he hit him because of "this" (pointing to a toy in his hand). The little boy's face was bleeding. I asked him whether it was okay if I took him home. He didn't seem to care. He seemed to be in his own little world trying to make sense of his life. So, I walked with him thinking that I have to see how I can help. At the same time, I knew that I couldn't get too involved, because I've found that when I get emotionally involved in a situation, I usually can't focus on the solution but get engulfed in a mess and can't be much help. So, one side of me was trying to handle the situating rationally, while my other side, my emotional side, was trying and wanting to just take the boy away from this.

We got to his home. I asked him if he could ask his mother to come to the door. He left quietly. His mother walked by him. They didn't even look at each other. She came to the door with a smile as if she'd known me for years. She asked me to come in, which is a not that uncommon in Iran; people tend to do that. I told her that I saw her son was beaten up by his dad and was there to see if there is something I could do to help with this situation. She didn't seem to understand that it was an issue, and why it was a concern. She just did not seem to get it. She was acting as if she was listening, but was emotionless. While I was stunned and angry, I tried to find compassion for her. It was hard, but I managed. I briefly explained to her what the hitting would do to her son, hoping that it would plant a seed of awareness.

Again, the struggle; one side of me wanted to take the boy out and shower him with gifts and spoil him and to take care of him, my other side knew that was the worst thing I could do, to give him a minute of fun and disappear. I knew I could not help him financially, I had done that before, and the father, who in many cases is a drug addict, uses the money for his own benefit. I knew there was nothing else I could do. After being stressed out for a while, I decided I needed to let go of the sadness and start focusing on what I can do to bring about any change.

I went back to my rule. I know I have an advocate and educator in me, and it is a passion of mine, so I decided to mix this side of me with the problem I witnessed to bring about a change, even if really slow, but I had to do something. I had seen too much and just could not sit and do nothing. Once I put that emotion into action, I started to feel better. I started a new foundation under my already existing foundation to bring awareness about child abuse in Iran. We started to find volunteers to translate articles about child abuse and hand them out to people, authorities, and parents. We started to have free seminars on the subject. For lower income families, we would give them free lunch to join. We just wanted them to hear it. To hear the damages they are creating. Maybe, just maybe, there is still a side of them that is connected to that essence, and that side will be awakened by hearing about it, now or later. We also decided to approach the authorities to change laws and implement those that exist about child abuse.

I use this example to show how we can use our emotions to get signals necessary to come up with a solution. Becoming overwhelmed by emotion is not the solution, since that is not what emotions and feelings are intended for.

I wrote these poems after witnessing this sad event.
Compassion

I feel your pain, I see that cane
I sense your wound, I hear your moan
I suffer from your sorrow
I carry on your horror
I believe your story
I gaze at your glory
I touch your soul
Your deepest core

I gaze into your eyes
I take a deep sigh
I see your heart
I feel your warmth

I wish I could turn into a thousand pieces
I wish I could save you and bring many ceases
I wish there was no more suffering
I wish I could be your buffering

Children

Sometimes I can't help but wonder
Why some children are torn asunder

Why they come to life only to suffer
There seems to be no break, it only gets tougher

Would they ever have hope?
How would they be able to cope?

Will they be able to grow?
How will they learn and know?

Will they even feel joy?
Will they ever have a toy?

Will they ever hear the word "love"?
Will they ever sense being "proud of"?

Questions pour, one after the other
I do have a side to me that is a mother

But I can't get engulfed in the emotion
The best I can do is to be a drop in the ocean

A drop of change, a sense of devotion
Even if the process is a slow motion

We are getting closer to an era of an awareness in which we can actually see how every action creates a reaction, and how we are all interconnected. On a daily basis, we are planting different seeds or nurturing those that already exist. These could be productive seeds or poisonous ones. If we want to learn about the mechanism of how things work, a good way is to plant a seed and watch it grow. We can even do a little experiment, comparing a number of seeds. We will notice that the more time, knowledge, love, and effort we put into growing the seed, the better plant we will have. So, our focus and effort created something beautiful (if done right). Now, the seed existed, so we didn't create from nothing, but we were the one who turned the seed into a fruitful plant.

In addition, we are getting closer to an era of an awareness in which we can see how we are all inner connected. The more expanded our mind gets, the more we see this connection.

Global Harmony

In order for the world to come to reconciliation
Nations need to have a solid foundation

Everyone has to learn a sense of cooperation
All have to feel they are a part of creation

Negativity is created by aggravation
Aggravation produces isolation

The world has to come to realization
That we all have an obligation

To work toward a global transformation
With communication, collaboration, determination

As I said, we are planting seeds continuously. First we have thoughts, emotions, and feelings, which may then lead us to some sort of action. The action by itself may lead to other actions. We keep on planting multiple seeds from the original one, since plants germinate and make copies of themselves, so we need to think about how we want to plant our seed.

Let's go a little farther from making philosophical comments and show how practical this can be. For example, our thought starts judging someone as bad or good based on some form of pre-assumption. If we are not in control of that thought and do not check its validity, the thought will turn into an action, perhaps a behavior, a judgmental look, a sarcastic phrase, a disrespectful act toward that individual. The individual may take it personally, and want to consciously or unconsciously defend herself. She may reflect your action by reacting. You experience what your thought created. You created that reaction in her. So, now, to make it worse, since you are not aware of your thought and therefore the root, you say to yourself, "See I was right, she is so mean."

In psychology, it is found that we put a lot of focus and energy into different means and methods to feel like our view of the world around us is correct. We will pick and choose only the information that supports our view and will totally shut down other perspectives. We do a filtration to make sure our comfort zone is not threatened. Evidence indicates that the more we hold on to a certain stereotyping, the more we remember information that supports that stereotype, related to that particular group. This is like a cycle in which the elements keep on feeding each other. For example, if we have strong belief that gay men are feminine, it is more likely that we will program ourselves with incidents that support this view. The Jew who is not into money, the Black who is articulate and intelligent, the White who is very caring, the Middle Eastern who is not a fanatic and ignorant, the Asian who speaks fluent English, the Hispanic who is well-educated and self-disciplined all become exceptions to the rule, and many times overlooked, but the rule is the same. In addition, we may look more intensely into the mistakes of a Black person in grammar, the spiritual beliefs a Middle Eastern person holds, etc.

When it comes to being an informed individual, one question pops up. Where is the information coming from? Did we create it, or has it been there all along and we simply found access to it? The Merriam-Webster online dictionary defines information as communication or reception of knowledge or intelligence, knowledge obtained from investigation, study or instruction, the attribute inherent in and communicated by one of two or more alternatives, sequences, or arrangements of something (as nucleotides in DNA or binary digits in a computer program) that produce specific effects, a signal or character representing data.

So, let's think about this. It's clear that information already exists. We are just finding access to it and discovering it. For example, nucleotides in DNA have always existed; we only discovered them. We have also discovered that DNA is a nucleic acid that has genetic instructions which are used as the basis of all organisms and some viruses. The main role of DNA is to store information. It is like a code that has instructions that are needed to build other components of cells. DNA is made from nucleotides. Now, as we said, this information has always been there, as long as there has been an organism. But it wasn't until science advanced that this information was discovered. So, the scientist who discovered this did not create it. The scientist simply put in an effort, knowledge, and determination into something she had a passion for, and found access.

As we are advancing from the primitive stage of mind, we are becoming more open to the fact that just because our five senses do not sense something, that does not mean it doesn't exit. There is whole wide world out there ready to be discovered. It would be such a waste to just sit and deny instead of reaching out and finding out. We need to discover what is within and what is outside.

To get to a place of having passion for learning, we need to ask ourselves these questions. Are we learning to release what no longer serves us? Any previously held thought, behavior, or emotion that is not being productive anymore? Do we have any worries, fears, self-doubts, anxious attachments, unreasonable expectations, and negative feelings toward someone that we are carrying with us? If so, how can we find ways to let them go and lighten up?

Do we really want to find the secret? The secret is us. Discovering what lies within us will be the door to the secret. Here are some ideas to start the process. See what works for you, and learn about them. Every one of these tips will lighten our baggage a little bit. To use a little of an Eastern metaphor, with each step we take toward releasing the unneeded energy and cleaning the dust of our existence, the clearer our mirror of being becomes, and we will become a true reflection of our selves. So, time to get to cleaning that mirror.

1. See what childhood patterns are still affecting your life. Learn about them, acknowledge them, process them, release them, and move on.

2. See what defenses your psyche is using to deal with life's matters. Psychological defenses range from primitive to advanced. Learn about them and see which ones you may use. Remember, the camera is on you. Come back!

3. Check and recheck what you're thinking pattern is. Is it rational and based on facts, or have you been imitating others without really knowing why? Are they working for you, or are they blocking your growth? Are they creating resentment, anger, hate, dislike, or other negative feelings? If so, how can you challenge them? Learn about rational vs. irrational thinking and self-reflect.

4. Do you have a set of values that are based on who you are, or are you chasing someone else's values? Do you know why you have the values you do? Are you focused on and clear about the goals and passions

of your life? If yes, what are they? If not, what is blocking you?

5. Are you self-reflecting at least three or more times every day? If not, why not? If yes, can you improve it?
6. Do you think you have expanded since one month ago, and is your answer going to be yes when you are asked this question one month from now? Are you a part of this continuous process, or are you struggling with your daily life every day?
7. Do you find a way to feel connected to nature daily, something supreme, some form of beautiful energy, in the form of prayer, mediation, or whatever works for you? If not, why not? If yes, how is it helping you with the learning and relaxing process? Again, check to make sure it is not imitation, but what you really want. Imitation is okay, if it works for you. It's okay to learn what works for others and check it out. During your prayer or meditation, do you show gratitude to remind yourself of the positive in your life? Do you pay attention to how insignificant you are, while at the same time how much value has been put onto you as this complex design with free will? Do you feel like bending down with this beauty? Do you use words of acknowledgment to remind yourself of how pure and magnificent this being you are admiring is?
8. Are you trying to learn something every day, based on a trusted source of knowledge? Whether it is history, culture, different religions, politics, places, countries, people, biology, chemistry, psychology, or physics, etc., can you see that all of these make you who you are and are a part of you, and can help you expand?

9. Are you working on becoming more and more aware and focusing on the moment? Are you learning to let go of past baggage and future worries while you are focused on the present, trying to have contentment, be productive, and find solutions for your life's obstacles?
10. Are you finding a balance between your mind and psyche's elements and getting one step closer to your wholeness?
11. Are you trying to face new things in life with a sense of responsibility, accountability and knowledge?
12. Detoxify your core by resting your mind through quiet time, refrain from any kind of negative/obsessive/addictive thoughts, emotions, and behaviors one day per week, stimulating your rational self-talk to drive toxic thoughts from your mind, encouraging removal of emotional waste and toxins through self-reflection, environmental filtration, and replacement, improving circulation of emotions and their harmony with thoughts and behavior, refueling the mind with reliable knowledge, positive thought, and connecting with nature.

So now the question is, where is my place in this world?

I was born in Iran, and moved to US when I was about 19. Therefore, at this point, from a nationality point of view, I am an Iranian-American. The positive side is that I have been able to live in two different countries from two different sides of the world. That has helped me grow in ways that might not have been possible if I'd had one but not the other; one rich in history and culture, and the other rich in technology, science, and a moderate level of freedom. I say moderate because once we fall slaves to the manipulating effects of external factors, we may not have as much freedom as we think we do.

After learning and experiencing my culture, my religion, and whatever else I was born into, I have learned to go above and beyond them. I have tried to live with the basic value that nothing I hold will be a tool of self-limitation but one of self-expansion. At this point, after walking through many phases of adjustment which brought insecurities, fear of unknowns, anxiety, and all else, I feel like I have an internal sense of liberation and can belong to any group, if I have that inner connection. Nothing external will hold me back, consciously or unconsciously. I am reaching a place where I am finally able to see things from a broader perspective, above and beyond my life's conditioning. It seems to be moving more and more from a selfish position to a collective one. My religion, my culture, my family, my education, my success, and my nationality and everything else I have been steeped in or gathered throughout my life, are a part of a package given to me for growth. It am not what I hold, but what I do with what I hold that makes me of value, and my goal is to make sure I use what is productive, and release what does not work anymore. I have set myself to refuse being taken as a slave. I have decided to become my own life's designer while I am trying to be fully aware of what it may offer. Synchronicity has proven itself to me on many occasions, and it continues to do so as my awareness evolves.

I have learned to be aware of subjectivity, and if possible become more and more objective. I find myself being more able to see the truth of what is, weaknesses and strengths, what works and what does not, which starts from myself, to my relationships, my nationality, and my religious background, and all other factors. I can see the truth more. It is, once again, nothing but a self-liberating experience. I have come to realize that there are too many selfish and subjective perceptions in today's world, and my experience with the two worlds is that usually those who know the least are the most opinioned about a subject. These are the type of people who don't want to hear the truth. No matter how factual the information, they shut down and get defensive. They are not receptive to anything that is different from their narrow perception of the world. They expect everything to work from their focal point of existence. If something resists that, they form negative feelings or actions toward it.

Ignorance gives me pain just as much as awareness gives me joy. I have found myself having more intense feelings, but at the same time having more ability to manage them and not being engulfed by them.

At this point, my hope is that globally we will get to a level of collective acceptance and learn to work together. I am hoping that realizing that simple fact will help us understand that if we don't get there, all of us will be damaged by it. Some sooner, some later, but none of us can escape. That understanding can create change. Change is what we need. Not a circular change but a moving upward toward expansion and growth.

At the end, if we feel like we are swimming in an ocean with no water, visiting an art exhibit that has no art in it, walking in a forest with no trees, looking at a sky with no stars, living in a no-depth zone and searching a state of nothingness; we might want to take a detour. It is never too late to take a detour, if only we can admit that we are lost.

Point of Reference

Self Actualization

Self-actualization is a process first described by a psychologist named Maslow. It is at the top of the self growth pyramid of growth. There have been some additions to the term since then, but in general, it refers to people who welcome reality and facts rather than rejecting the truth, who have high peak experiences, and are relatively tolerant of themselves and others.

It seems that humans have a natural tendency toward self-actualization in order to develop their potential, so that they feel an enhanced sense of self. This natural tendency encourages a sense of equilibrium within the person. An equilibrium that gives the person a sense of inner peacefulness.

Self-actualization is considered to be a more mature way of comprehending life as it unfolds. Self-actualized individuals seem to have a sense of purpose in life, genuine interpersonal relationships that are meaningful and focused on quality not quantity, consequential activities, logical ways of thinking, an understanding and responsiveness to their emotions, ability to identify with higher human values, and self-respect.

Individuals functioning at this level seem to have moved

beyond the ego-oriented needs of Maslow's hierarchy to identify more with their sense of higher self. Further, these individuals tend to focus most of their time in the present while having clear plans for the future. They have learned ways to cope with past memories that might have been negative, letting go of the resentments and anger or any other negative emotions related to these memories. They also plan ahead for their future but don't get engulfed into the negative emotions it may bring like unreasonable worry.

They seem to see life as a continuum, and seem to be more aware of how their life is unfolding and how it is evolving toward a profound purpose, resulting in a more logical acceptance of what is to come.

Self actualized people seem to be more in tuned with reality as it unfolds rather than living in a fantasy world with unrealistic expectations and constant struggle to satisfy basic needs. They tend to have inner-directed, independent, and self-supportive behaviors. They are interested in moving forward in life rather than waling in a circular path. They seem to have less need for approval from other people because they have found ways to accept themselves. They accept all of themselves, strengths or weaknesses, and have found a way to understand that only with acceptance change is possible. They understand that no one can change by being in denial and seem to function from a more advanced psychological system including more mature defenses.

Self actualized humans do not function based on other people's perceptions but only those of themselves. They are not followers and do not imitate others, they only learn from what is logical. This does not mean that they are not concerned and neither does it mean that they are not connected with other peoples' matters, but it does mean that their decisions are made from their own core of consciousness and based on knowledge. People who have been able to get to this level of maturation follow their own inner vision, have fewer needs and anxious attachments, are not very concerned with results but with learning and experience, have their own definition of what is productive for them, and are aware of the choices and the effect these choices have on them and the world. They are willing to take responsible risks if that helps with their growth process.

The main blockages to self-actualization are fear of challenge, irrational beliefs, lack of knowledge about self and surroundings, limiting conditionings, and the inability to apply the knowledge to make the self grow intellectually, emotionally, mentally, and spiritually.

To deal with the fear of challenges, we should understand that like all other emotions fear in balanced form is useful for our survival and development. Therefore, in the right capacity, fear is an emotion we need but too much of it can prevent us from doing things that might be necessary or productive for our life. There are rational and irrational fears. For example, fear of snakes is a rational fear that keeps us safe from being hurt by them. However, we have to learn ways to let go of our irrational fears. This can be accomplished by learning the root of the fear, visualizing how our life will change if we challenge that irrational fear; challenging the irrationality with more rational ways of thinking, and finally facing the fear. Reasonable fear is a necessity, unreasonable fear is an obstruction.

When it comes to self-actualization, behaviors that go against the individual's actualizing predisposition generate inadequacy in the sense of self. Individuals sometimes use defenses to escape the fear or discomfort they may face in their lifetime. They may twist perceptions of reality to reduce what they see as a threat, or they can act in ways that avoid becoming aware of the threatening experiences, for example by ignoring or denying it.

We can see people who blame their failures on causes outside themselves while crediting themselves for their successes. These behaviors may lead to self-handicapping strategies that prevent the individual from walking away from that which is unproductive, staying in the comfort zone even if it does not serve her anymore.

This by itself creates the inability to move up the ladder of self growth.

Self actualized individuals are followers of their own essence and create a healthy life for themselves and as a result have the ability to give back more to the world naturally and innately.

Attachment vs. Love; Peace vs. Happiness

Let's explain four key words: attachment, love, peace, and happiness. Attachment can be defined as a warm bond that forms between one person and another. This bonding ties the two together in space and continues over time. Attachment to something or someone that is positive for us, up to the point of being able to let go when we should, is healthy. But if we don't find a balance in the way we're attached, it may turn into dependency and go even further into obsession which is damaging.

Love can be defined as an essential element of a person's experience, which can include a sense of affection, an attraction, self-sacrifice, and a sense of connection to nature, other living things, and ultimately to some superior being. A true sense of love is essential in the process of self-identification.

Peace is achieved when an individual's different components are in harmony, a person is in control of her emotions, thoughts, and behaviors; and feels and accepts them as they come, and the person is aware of her state of being and her moments. This is a very personal experience, which can only be realized through a person's knowledge of self and her experience of life. This experience cannot be achieved by imitation, because something that works for someone else does not necessarily mean that it will work for another. This is why we witness many people going to mosque, church, and other spiritual gatherings, reading all kinds of books on spirituality, and never changing their negative patterns of behavior, emotion, or thought; or they may change one negative behavior and replacing it with another. They also seem unaware of their impact on the world.

We can learn from other people's experiences and it is always essential to gather new reliable source of information and to stimulate our mind. But we need to mold this knowledge to our own situations, strengths, weaknesses, and potentials. Peace can also be defined as the absence of hostilities, negative thoughts, and ongoing damaging emotions. It is an internal experience not an external persona or set of behaviors.

To define the term happiness, it is an emotional state defined as a feeling of satisfaction. Happiness is needed to feel a sense of peace. A true state of happiness is a personal matter and how it is defined is dependent on the level of maturity the person is in. The opposite side of happiness is unhappiness, but they are not separate entities; they are different areas of the same spectrum. They feel, however, quiet different. In psychology, a definition of happiness focuses on three areas: feeling good, having positive thoughts toward life, and not feeling bad. It is a general sense of satisfaction and looking forward to what is yet to come. In this view, there is no specific definition of happiness. It seems to be related to both quantity and quality of life, which again are personal determinations.

Too many people look for quantity to feel happy and respond quickly to their impulses to have a temporarily sense of satisfaction, which they identify as happiness. But looking to find happiness through temporarily satisfactions may leave the person wanting to gain more to feel the same or even less. Sometime the cost outweighs the benefit but being unaware makes the whole process ongoing and repeating itself. The person may invest a long time gaining something for a relatively short feeling of happiness. Besides that looking for a true sense of happiness through outside world can be overwhelming and confusing since there is so much.

Psychological Defenses

Psychological defense mechanisms are an important aspect of a person's mental growth that he or she must become familiar with. These are psychological strategies that individuals use to cope with the reality of life and to maintain their self-image in one piece. All of us use many different defenses during our lifetimes but these become pathological if they're used all the time, and lead to maladaptive behaviors that threaten the person's wellbeing.

We have pathological, immature, neurotic, and mature types of defenses. Pathological defenses are those that prevent the person from being able to deal with a real threat and to see reality clearly. An example of this would be a person who is so deeply in denial that there she may have a problem, a controlling husband who says his marriage is great, an alcoholic who says she is not addicted to alcohol, a person who keeps on making the same mistakes over and over again and blames others etc.

An immature type of defense is the one used in childhood and adolescence but mostly discarded in adulthood since they may lead to socially unacceptable behavior. As children and teenagers we can't see reality as it really is. We see the surface part of everything, people, places etc. But as we grow, our ability to comprehend should be growing. If we're being nurtured in a healthy environment, our psychological defenses should become more evolved.

The other type of defense, which is neurotic, is the one that does not deal with reality and can cause many problems in all areas of life, especially in interrelationships and enjoying life. And the fourth type of defense, which is the mature defense, is used by mentally healthy adults.

We can put defenses into levels according to severity of problems they may cause in the person. Level 1 defense is the ones that are almost always pathological because the person uses them to rearrange external reality so she will not have to deal with them. These are denial, distortion, and delusional projection. An example of denial is a person who refuses to accept reality. We see people who deny they have a problem, despite the obvious signs of having one. For example, a father who blames his bad relationship with his children as being his ex wife's fault without having factual information to support this. The next one is distortion, which is when someone reshapes external reality to meet her internal needs. An example of this would be a wife who is extremely unhappy in her marriage but will reshape her reality of what she sees in a way to be able to get some form of satisfaction which is unseccsufful. In the next defense, delusional projection, one projects her inner blockages onto the other. An example of this is a person who suffers from extreme anger and sees everyone else threatening her in an angry way.

The second group of defense mechanisms includes fantasy, projection, hypochondria, and passive-aggressive behaviors. This group of defenses is used by many adults and adolescents. If one just uses them every once in a while, these may adjust distress and anxiety imposed by other people or the real world. However, for those who use these on a regular basis, they are considered to be immature defenses, and lead to serious problems in the person's ability to cope with the real world.

In fantasy, people draw back into fantasy to resolve inner and outer conflicts. For example, these people would go into a made-up and imaginary world to escape their problems, rather than concentrating on a solution. In projection, the person blames another for her feelings. Prejudice and severe jealousy may come from this type of defense. In the passive-aggressive type of defense, the person expresses her aggression toward another indirectly and passively. In the last defense, which is acting-out behavior, the person directly expresses an unconscious wish or impulse to avoid being conscious of the emotion that goes with that impulse. For example, a person who is very angry and acts out in an angry way may have some very painful emotions that she is trying to hide, because she is not ready to face them.

Then comes level three of the defense mechanisms. These are fairly common in adults, and many normally functioning adults use them. These may have short-term benefits but used too often and for too long they can create long-term problems in relationships and daily life and enjoying life in general. These are intellectualization, repression, reaction formation, displacement, and distortion.

Intellectualization is when one tries to separate oneself from emotions, it is a form of just thinking not acting. Repression is when the emotion is conscious but the idea that is behind it is absent. For example, I am feeling really sad, but I w ill not think about it. Reaction formation is when one acts completely opposite to what one wants or feels, for example taking care of someone when one wants to be taken care of. This will or may work in short run, but will break down in the long run. The other defense at this level is displacement, which is separating an emotion and redirecting the intense emotion toward someone or something that is less unpleasant or threatening in order to avoid dealing with what is frightening or directly threatening. Another defense is dissociation, which is a temporary and extreme adjustment of one's personal identity or temperament to avoid emotional suffering.

Finally, the last level of defense, which is common among the most mentally healthy adults is the one in which the individual uses her defenses to master her pleasure and feelings, and to integrate many of the conflicting emotions and thoughts and still make them be effective. These are sublimation, altruism, control, anticipation, and humor. Sublimation is converting negative emotions into positive actions. This is an example of someone who turns her anger toward someone and does some kind things for another person. Altruism is when one gives constructive services to others that brings her a sense of satisfaction. Suppression is the conscious decision to postpone paying attention to an emotion or need in order to cope with the present reality, but then the emotion is attended to and processed at a later and more appropriate time. Anticipation is a realistic planning for future unpleasant events and humor is an over-expression of ideas and feelings that gives pleasure to others. At the end, the more mature and evolved a human being become, the more she is capable of functioning through the higher levels of defenses.

Maslow's pyramid of needs

Maslow states that humans are motivated by unsatisfied needs and that certain lower needs need be satisfied before higher needs can be attended. His concept indicates that the general needs of physiological, safety, love, and esteem have to be met and fulfilled before a person is able to act unselfishly. He categorizes these needs as deficiency needs and reports that until one satisfies these deficiency needs, whatever one does is selfish whether consciously or unconsciously aware of it.

Reasonable satisfaction of these needs are necessary while ignoring and denying them may create an illness or evil acts in a person. For adequate self discovery process, it is important that individuals understand which needs are active for them and what creates their motivation in life in order to understand their intentions behind their behavior. This will help them get more in tuned with their unconscious mind.

Maslow's model indicates that in general basic, low-level needs such as physiological requirements and safety must be satisfied before higher-level needs such as self-fulfillment are pursued. When a need is satisfied, it no longer motivates and the next higher need takes its place.

A brief description of these needs is:

Level 1: Biological and Physiological needs. Basic life needs like air, food, drink, shelter, warmth, sex, homeostasis, breathing, water, excretions, etc.

Level 2: Safety needs. Protection, security, order, law, limits, stability, personal security, financial security, health and well being, safety net against accidents/illness and adverse impacts.

Level 3: Belonging and love needs. Family, affection, relationships, work group, social/cultural/religious groups, friendship, intimacy, having a supportive and communicative groups to belong to, giving and receiving love.

Level 4: Esteems needs met by external factors. Achievement, status, responsibility, reputation, recognition, attention, social status.

Level 5: Esteems needs met by internal factors, accomplishment, self respect, an inner sense of contentment with one's self.

Level 6: Self Actualization. Personal growth and fulfillment, truth, justice, wisdom, meaning in life, peak experiences, energized, harmony, always finding opportunities to grow, striving for full potential, awareness of self. According to Maslow, only 2% of the population get to be self actualized not because they cannot but because they get stuck at fulfilling the lower needs.

Level 6 (deeper into it): Need for Aesthetics and knowledge. Maslow later added this as a part of self actualization but further down that level.

Level 7: Self Transformation. This is where the individual experiences the ultimate state of inner liberation being free from the concept of self and its conditioning into a state of selflessness; and living from being connected to something bigger. This is where the individual gets free from anxious attachments, neediness, irrational thinking, unbalanced emotions and impulses, and being dragged by the ego.

It is important to note that this pyramid and the experiences related to each level are different for different individuals. Different individuals may be capable of moving faster, slower, not at all, or jumping from one to the other depending on their unique personalities, abilities, limitations, strengths, and innately born talents. In addition, some individuals have the ability to replace an unmet need with something positive to fulfill its empty feeling.

<u>Other books by this author</u>

<u>Book 1:</u> There is one religion: The religion of KNOW THYSELF.

This book attempts to answer those seemingly ordinary questions of life with deep factual/practical answers. How do I get to my core being? Who am I? What do I do with my religion, culture, environment, family, gender, childhood etc., and how should I interact with these aspects of my identity? I feel like I have no use for some of these concepts. Do I need to learn about them, and if so, why? How do I put meaning to my life? What do I do with my emotional baggage? Others say I have it all, so why do I feel empty, sometimes? Why do I have such an emotional pain and can't cure it? I have so many people around me, so why do I feel lonely sometimes?

In this book there is a case example of an individual who learned about her culture, religion, and family background to ease her self-growth process. An individual who moved from East to West in her teen life, and used her immigration experience as a blessing, considering herself privileged to have had experienced living in two seemingly different countries in her lifetime..She came to learn that this experience had expanded her mind and thought in ways that would not have been possible if she had not immigrated. She also learned ways to learn and acknowledge the aspects of her life that she had escaped from, and found the experience fulfilling and uplifting. She felt a sense of having control over her life, picking what works, getting rid of whatever conditioning does not serve her, and choosing her own destiny.

Whatever we hold, we have to learn about and experience. Only after that we can make an informed decision about letting go of what does not work. If we let go of anything before learning and processing, we are getting ourselves into avoidance and repression rather than freedom. We can't ignore the rules and expect good results.

<u>Book 2:</u> Rumi & Self Psychology: The Psychology of Tranquility Rumi's Poetic Language vs. Carl Jung's Psychological Language.

This book focuses on some of Rumi's poems related to the concept of self. In addition, it discusses some of Carl Jung's Concepts of Psyche, self-discovery, self-actualization, self-liberation, self-determination, self-assertion, self-discipline, emotional stability, and self-knowledge.

Book 3: A Therapy Dialogue

A session-by-session therapy dialogue with an educated client who went through the self-actualization and self-growth processes. This book walks the reader through the process of therapy. In a step-by-step guide, it discusses what it means to live a life of "false self" and how to find a sense of "real self." It discusses a wide variety of issues like anxiety, family relationships, romantic relationships, negative behaviors and emotions and how to get rid of them, how to get to our full potential, what happiness really means, what is the difference between love and anxious attachment, what is assertiveness, how to process suppressed memories, and how to be able to see deeper into people's intentions, not just their behavior.

<u>Book 4:</u> A concise comparison of Carl Jung and Abraham Maslow's theoretical concepts.

Finding a common ground between Carl Jung's general concepts of individuation, wholeness, spirituality and religion and those of Maslow's including his self Actualization and homeostasis concepts. (Out in 2010)

SKBF Publishing www.SKBFPublishing.com

SKBF Publishing is a publishing company dedicated to providing educational information for enhancing lifestyles and helping to create a more productive world through more aware individuals. Our task is to help awareness overcome ignorance. Our publishing focus is on research-oriented and/or reliability books, including subjects related to education, parenting, self-improvement, psychology, spirituality, science, culture, finance, mental and physical health, and personal growth. We try to analyze each book carefully and to choose the books we feel have reliable and valid information, based on available research or the credentials of the author. Our team of experts reviews every manuscript submitted to us for its practicality and content.

Our mission is to publish information that expands understanding and promotes learning, compassion, self-growth, and a healthy sense of self which leads to a healthier lifestyle. Our vision is to make a difference in people's lives by providing informative material that is reliable and research-oriented. SKBF Publishing is honored to have the helping hand of a number of scientist, educators, researchers, intellectuals, and scholars working together to review the books before approval for publishing with *SKBF.*

About the Author

Dr. Rohani Rad has a Doctorate in Clinical Psychology and a Masters e in Applied Psychology. She is a member of American Psychological Association (APA), Virginia Psychological Association, and Applied Psychological Association.

In addition, she is the founder of a not-for-profit foundation (www.SelfKnowledgeBase.com) with the sole task of bringing root oriented awareness to a wide variety of subjects ranging from understanding of global peace to child abuse. This foundation aims to be a bridge of understanding between the East and the West by generating research-oriented material and bringing reliable information. Informed individuals make up an informed world.

Dr. Rad is also a researcher, and is actively involved with a number of studies related to emotional wellbeing, children's mental health, and relationships, among others. These studies are performed in both the Eastern and the Western sides of the globe for a broader perspective of factual information.

Dr. Rad has written a number of recognized and up-to-the-point books about the subjects of self-discovery, self-growth, and self-awareness from a psychological perspective. You can find more information about the author and her books on her website at www.OnlineHealthClinic.com